ERSILLIA:
Love & Loss

Based on a True Story

By

Stephen A. White

With

Kathleen Ersillia Anderson

Foreword

By Kathleen Ersillia Anderson

Ersillia is my middle name . . . a name I have always loved. Assad Hajjar and Frances Ersillia Galliotti were my grandparents. They immigrated to America to begin anew and create a better life for themselves and their children. My mother was Lydia Concetta, their youngest daughter.

My life's dream was always to write the story of my grandparent's love for each other, their life's journey that involved the Vatican, their taboo relationship, living on three continents as husband and wife and the joys and sadness of their existence.

While growing up my mother and her older sisters, Tecla and Inez, told me bits and pieces of their parent's story. It has always been in my mind and heart a love story between my grandparents that needed to be written. Unfortunately, all we had were the remnants of a story, a portrait painted only around the edges. I felt the time was now right to create the lives of my grandparents, to weave a tapestry—*based on actual world events*—that would allow the reader to imagine what their lives *might* have been like.

Hopefully, those who read this story will come to know and understand Frances and Assad, but especially Frances, and I hope that the reader's hearts will come to look kindly on them both.

My mother and my aunts' recanting of family information was not, however, an open book that they were willing to read aloud to the world. It was tinged with shame and humiliation by the tragic turn all their lives took when my grandmother committed a violent act in 1938; and even though my brother Robert and I would not be born for ten years, it directly affected our lives as well.

My brother and I were raised and blessed by the influence of these wonderful and strong women, especially my mother Lydia. All three eventually became proud American Citizens. They inspired the writing of this story. I hope you enjoy reading about their lives.

Note: In the spelling below, Hajjar was changed by Assad to Haggiar when living in Italy with the intent of Europeanizing the name.

Dedicated to my mother,

Lydia Concetta Haggiar Anderson

From the Author

On May 11, 2020, I received an email from Kathy Anderson. It was a long email, rather detailed, but what hooked me were the opening lines:

"I have lived with a family story in my head and mind for as long as I can remember. It involves the church, taboo relationships, murder, happiness and sadness and other human emotions. Can you help me? Do you think it makes a good novel?"

Are you kidding? It was like waving catnip in from of a kitty's face. I was hooked. I asked Kathy to paint me a picture of everything she knew about her family, as best she could. She did, bless her heart. But when she was done she presented me with a canvas painted ***only around the edges***. I knew the names of family members. I knew approximately when they were born. I knew the four continents they traveled from, and approximately when those journeys occurred. But that was it.

So taking what information I had, coupled with my love of world history, I then proceeded to fill in the rest of the painting, using as my palette actual world events and historic figures that may have *possibly* intersected with the real-life "leaves" on Kathy's family tree. And, if so, determining *how* they would have interacted *and* reacted with the history unfolding around them.

ERSILLIA: Love & Loss spans 70 years and travels nearly halfway around the world in telling its story. Hopefully, as Kathy touched upon in her email, it contains all the elements of a good novel. You be the judge.

Stephen A. White

CHAPTER ONE

May 1885

The Mediterranean Sea

Just South of the Greek Isles

Is the man going to die, mama? What's wrong with him?

Assad Hajjar can hear the question as he lay on his dirty cot in the ship's hold; his mind glazed over by a scorching fever that causes him to shiver so violently it feels like every joint in his body is coming loose. He thinks it is the voice of a young girl, maybe seven or eight years old, but he can't be sure. At almost six feet, two inches, his legs partially hang over the edge of the cot. Despite the ravishing of his body, his face is strong and full, with a thick handlebar mustache partially covering his upper lip, his hair thick and black. Suddenly, his body spasms as he leans over and vomits into a pail. The ache comes in waves from his head to his toe.

Lying back on the cot, Assad barely remembers the last few days, no more than pictures fading in and out. What he does remember is that he is on a merchant ship, crowded and filthy; too many people, too little space. Upon boarding the ship he was instantly appalled at what he had seen. The lower section of the ship was a miserable hole, full of dirt and filth, where the men and women and children are packed like sardines. Assad could see it right away with the extremely dirty and lazy habit of the men themselves, allowing filth of all kinds to accumulate all over the ship, without taking the slightest trouble to remove it. Conditions were made worse by the cook who, instead of throwing refuse over the side of the ship, merely used it to fortify the remaining food, while potatoes soaked in filthy water. No attention was paid by the captain to the sanitary state of the ship, making it all a breeding ground for…

Cholera, Anya. I think he has cholera.

What is… cholera?

It's a very bad sickness. Your grandmamma told me about it, how when she was a little girl, about your age, everyone in her village suddenly got sick. People started to die, many people; men, women, children, little babies in their cradles. One night men came on horses from the city and made everyone, even my

8

mother, leave their village and everything they had. After everyone was gone they set fire to all the homes. She could never go back.

That makes me sad, mama. I don't want the man to die. He's been good to us on this trip. He saved me.

I know, Anya... I know. But don't worry, I don't think God would abandon one of his own.

Assad feels a cool cloth placed on his head. It temporarily dulls the pain and lessens the fire in his body long enough to let thoughts and memories float back to the surface of his subconscious. A different place and time. Ten long years ago. It's where a 12-year old boy from Altou, a small village in Lebanon nestled at the foot of a mighty mountain, where tall cedar trees seem to rise and kiss the clouds, would share an evening meal with his mother and father. A memory far away from the pain and the suffering closing in on him as the ship pitches back and forth on the rough Mediterranean Sea.

Assad sees his home. It is small, only four rooms, but meticulously clean. The house is warm from a fireplace that also serves to cook the evening's dinner. Assad is sitting at a wooden table reading a school book. His father, also named Assad, is a tall man, barrel-chested, with a long dark beard showing flecks of gray. He has just come in from washing outside but Assad can still smell the shavings from the cedar planks he uses to make the furniture that he takes to Beirut to sell to wealthy landowners. He kisses his wife, Tillie, as she begins to serve dinner. The smell is glorious, filling all corners of the house.

It is Assad's favorite meal; a meat pie made from minced lamb and cracked wheat, served with a salad made from parsley, tomatoes, and burghul, a mixture of ground cinnamon and mint. Assad's father drinks *arak*, a strong licorice-flavored liquor made from fermented grape juice. When he mixes it with water and ice it turns white. Assad has milk. Momma drinks water. Before eating, the family holds hands around the table and begins to pray to Jesus for the modest bounty placed in front of them. As Christians, it is what they have done before each meal. It is something they have done since as far back as Assad can recall. And it has always brought him a sense of comfort and peace. But not on this night.

No sooner had they said their "Amen's," when there's a violent pounding on the door, so loud it make Assad's momma spill her water. Assad can see the veins and muscles in his father's neck coil like springs, as his face begins to darken. The pounding continues, louder and louder, a deep voice booming from the other side.

"OPEN THE DOOR, ASSAD! YOU KNOW WHY I'M HERE!"

Look, Mama. Why does his face move like that?

I think he is having a bad dream. It must be from the fever.

Mama, tell me again, where are we going? And when will we get there; this ship smells yucky.

Soon, Anya, maybe in a few more days. We're going somewhere very different, with new people who will speak differently than us. Where, hopefully, we will be happy.

When he gets feeling better, can the man come with us, Mama?

We'll see. We'll see. Please hand me another wet cloth. I think his fever is starting to pass.

That makes me happy. Mama, how do you think he got that scar over his eye?

As Assad's father rises to answer the door, the tension pours off him like water; the room actually seeming to shrink. When he opens the door he glares at the man standing there, who is wearing a small smile that curls on the edge of his thick lips. He is short, fat, but not soft-looking. His bullet-shaped head sits on his shoulders, literally, as he appears to have no neck. He holds what appears to be a ledger in one hand, and a menacing-looking baton in the other. Assad has seen the man around the village, talking to neighbors, threatening them with the baton, often in the company of three or four equally unpleasant yet very large men. His name is Salim Al-Mahoud, and he is of the religious order known as the Druze. Assad remembers sitting with his father at night by the fireplace, watching as he lit his pipe with a twig, the aroma of the tobacco wafting throughout the house. And he would hear of terrible times.

The villagers called it the Mount Lebanon Civil War, which occurred in 1860 when Christian peasants began an uprising just north of Mount Lebanon, targeting their Druze overlords. The rebellion soon spread to the south of the country, where the fighting became even fiercer. When the fighting finally wound down, around 20,000 Christians were killed by the Druze, with 380 Christian villages and 560 churches destroyed. The Druze also suffered heavy casualties. And in just over 15 years since, both religions had maintained a tenuous peace. But now, sitting at his kitchen table, watching both men stare at each other like male rams vying for the attention of the lone female in the flock, Assad thinks that peace looks brittle at best.

"What do you want, Salim Al-Mahoud?"

The smile curled even further up the stout man's lip. "You know what I want, Assad. I see all the trips you take to Beirut with your furniture. I know you are making a very profitable living."

"I told you before, that is none of your business," Assad's father replies through gritted teeth. "We have nothing to talk about."

"Ah, but we do, my friend." Al-Mahoud enters the kitchen, stops, and tosses the ledger on the table, knocking over Assad's glass of milk, the liquid running off the table and on to the floor. "Do you think it's a coincidence that you make that journey to Beirut, back and forth, and never once get robbed by bandits? It is only because I, Salim Al-Mahoud, deem it to be so. And for that protection, I expect appropriate compensation, which I see—tapping the baton on the ledger—you have not paid me."

"And I won't. Now leave this house."

Moving surprisingly fast for a short man, with a wide sweep of the baton Al-Mahoud sends everything on the table crashing to the floor. Assad heard his mother gasp, watching in horror as dishes left to her by her mother and her mother before her, shatter on the floor, broken pieces scattering in all directions. "You *will* pay me what I am owed," Al-Mahoud bellows. "Or I will come back and burn this house to the ground! And everyone in it!"

Now enraged, not only by the sight of smashed heirlooms but threats to his family, the younger Assad leaps from his chair and furiously lashes out at the stocky man, his fingers aiming for the pudgy face. But the attack is too slow and Al-Mahoud strikes Assad over his eye with the baton. The pain explodes in Assad's skull as blood quickly spurts from the gash, dripping into his eyes. But even through the dripping red haze, Assad can make out his father moving swiftly towards his assailant, his fist cocked. Before Al-Mahoud can react, his father delivers a staggering punch to the face of the man, whose lips split, several teeth flying from his mouth. The force of the blow forces Al-Mahoud to stagger and fall, the side of his head striking the edge of the cast-iron stove with a sickening thud. He crumbles to the floor. Gasps gurgled from his throat, his chest heaved once, twice, then no more.

Assad's father looks down at the dead man, seemingly stunned by the sudden outburst of violence, albeit in defense of his family. Assad's mother walks over to him, taking his hand in hers. They look at each other, and then at the body on the floor. "Oh, Assad. What's to become of us now?" Her voice is shaking. "You know what's going to happen. His men will come looking for him. How can we protect ourselves against such an army?"

"We can't, woman. But we must protect our son."

Although Assad, now holding a bloody towel to his forehead, doesn't completely understand what his father is saying, he can see by his mother's eyes that *she* does understand. And what she understands is horrifying to her.

"You want to send our son away? But where will he go, where will he possibly be safe from these horrible men?"

"One of the families that purchases our cedar tables is a caretaker at the Monastery of Saint Anthony of Qozhaya in the Qadisha Valley, just a few hours journey from here," says Assad's father, gripping both his mother's hands and looking intently into her tear-filled eyes. "This man, he is good friends with the abbot. I am sure if we send him there they will guide his path. The monastery is surrounded by forests of pine and cedar and orchards that can only be reached by a narrow, winding road. Assad will be safe there."

Assad is horrified at the thought of leaving his parents. "No, I won't go! I will stay and fight with you!" He fights back the tears but he can see the resolve in his father's face. "You must go, Assad, it is the only way to keep you safe. We can take care of ourselves. But *only* if we know you are safe."

Wrapping his arms tightly around his father's waist, the pain is almost unbearable. "Please Papa." Placing his large hand on his son's head, Assad's father bends down and whispers in his ear, "Go my son, and become the best man you can be. Help others. Keep your faith strong. And always remember how much we love you."

A 12-year old Assad Hajjar cannot control the sobs wracking his body.

Mama, I think the man is crying. Look, I can see tears.

Whatever he is remembering must be horrible, Anya. Come, let us pray for him.

To Assad, caught in the tightening grip of cholera, the voices he hears are becoming clearer. He thinks it sounds like a small girl and an older woman; her mother, perhaps? But who was crying? What did they mean? As he starts to raise his head from the pillow to get a closer look, a pain shoots through his stomach like a hot poker. Assad writhes in pain, wretches several times, than falls back on the pillow, spent and soaked with sweat. And the memories once again flood over him.

CHAPTER TWO

April 1895

Monastery of Saint Anthony of Qozhaya

Two days before setting sail from Lebanon to Italy

Sitting in his bare room at the monastery, surrounded by the minimal amount of conveniences—a hard bed, bureau, nightstand—a now 22-year old Assad Hajjar, having recently been ordained a Catholic priest, thinks back on how swiftly the 10 years have passed, and how much he has missed his mother and father. There had been no communication since he left his home that night. That was the plan. All efforts were made so that no one, especially Al-Mahoud's men, could find him. Assad didn't even know if his parents were still alive. His heart ached at the thought they may have been murdered. Sitting on the edge of the bed, the Bible on his lap opened to Psalm 71:14-16, Assad whispers the words:

But I will keep hope alive, and my praise to You will grow exponentially.
I will bear witness to Your merciful acts; throughout the day I

will speak of all the ways You deliver, although, I admit, I do
not know the entirety of either.

I will come with stories of Your great acts, my Lord, the
Eternal. I will remind them of Your justice, only Yours.

His praying is quickly interrupted by a soft knock on the door. Assad rises from the bed and places the Bible on the nightstand, careful to mark his page with a scrap of paper. He walks over and opens the door.

"I hope I am not disturbing you, my son," says the elderly man in the doorway, who is dressed in a long robe, the sleeves just a tad too long for his thin arms. His face is lean and drawn, but his eyes twinkle and his lips seem always ready for a smile. His beard is long and white, but carefully trimmed.

"Of course not, Father Abbot," Assad replies, opening the door wider to allow the abbot to enter the room. "I am blessed by your presence. Is something wrong?"

The abbot slowly walks over to the bed and sits down. Silently, the old man stares down at his hands, now firmly clasped together. "Again I ask, Father Abbot, respectfully, is something wrong?"

Still seated, the abbot looked up at Assad. He smiled softly, but it is not an expression of happiness. Could someone actually smile and still be in pain, Assad wondered?

"Ten long years ago you came to us in the dark of night, a frightened boy, lost and alone. But we all watched you grow into an incredible young man, one who saw his calling and embraced the teachings of our Savior."

"It would never have been possible without your guidance, and all those within these walls," said Assad, trying hard to read what was unfolding in the old man's mind.

"We knew why you had come, what your father had done to protect his family from a man like Salim Al-Mahoud, a man who has a hole in his black heart, a hole that can only be filled by the misery and pain and suffering of others. That is why we forgave your father for his actions." The abbot paused and rubbed his eyes. Assad thought he looked weary and drawn, as if struggling all day to make the right decision, a decision that was resting on his frail shoulders like bags of crushed gravel. Again he looked at Assad and smiled. "You have grown into a fine young man; tall, strapping, well-conditioned. You will do well, with our Lord's help, on your journey."

Assad was confused. "Journey? What journey? I don't understand." He knelt down on one knee in front of the abbot. "Am I to leave the monastery? But why? Have I offended the Order; have I offended *you*?"

The abbot took both of Assad's hands in his, squeezing them gently. "You could never offend me, my son," he said. "But men like Salim Al-Mahoud, and those who have followed him blindly over the years, will never stop searching for you. It is what drives them. It is their misguided fuel. They will be relentless. And, they *will* find you."

"But," Assad stammered, "its been 10 years. Surely they no longer care about a 12-year old boy who ran away from… his parents," the last words came out softly, slowly; the memory still raw.

"Alas, if it were only true," said the abbot wearily. "But we have heard tales that they are starting to ask more and more questions about you. They will come soon. And as abbot, I am sworn to protect this monastery." The abbot looked away. "I am sorry, but you must leave."

Assad stood and paced the room. His mind racing, looking for answers that he could not comprehend. "But, but, where will I go? How will I travel? Where can I possibly be safe anywhere in Lebanon from men such as these? Should I go to Syria, and hide there like a common criminal? How will I practice my faith… how will I spread His teachings? *Tell me, Father Abbot.*"

"No, you must leave this area all together and go far away, if you are to stay safe," the abbot answered, his voice now stronger than at any time since he first entered Assad's room. "You will travel to Italy, to Rome, the very seat of our Holy Faith, under the protection of his Holiness, Pope Leo XIII, praise his name."

Assad stopped pacing and stared at the abbot, trying to comprehend what he had just said. Italy? Assad had heard of such a country mentioned by his father once or twice, and as a priest he certainly knew the existence of the Holy Father. But Assad had no concept of exactly where Italy was. What he did know, however, was that it lay far across a great body of water, likely many days journey by ship. Assad's mind started to reel. Where would he get a ship, and how would he pay for passage? It was all too much to work out in his brain. His head started to ache. He subconsciously rubbed the scar over his eyebrow.

The abbot, who is very wise, could see what Assad was thinking and that he was struggling with questions that seemingly had no answers. He told Assad what the plan was.

"There is a businessman I am familiar with, a man by the name of Captain Giovanni Galliotti," the abbot explained. "He is a rich Italian merchant living in Sicily. He earns much money through his olive groves in Italy and a small fleet of merchant ships that he uses to transport cedar planks from the docks at Beirut to the Port of Messina, at the southern tip of Italy. He is in Beirut now and set to return to Italy in two days. Occasionally, along with his cargo, he will also take with him, for a fee of course, passengers who are looking to start a new life in a new land. It's a rough journey, perhaps up to a week at sea under the harshest of conditions. But sometime this is what people will pay for the price of freedom and a fresh start. That is where you will start your new life. Captain Galliotti is aware that you will be a passenger on his ship when it sets sail in two days. He is tough but a good man."

The abbot rose and walked out of the room. The last thing Assad hears is, "Go, my son, with our blessings."

Why do you think the man is on this ship, mama?

I don't know, Anya, he never really said. But it is not our place to pry into his private business.

Okay, mama, I understand. Can I give him some water in a cup?

Yes, I think he might like that.

The pain has subsided enough that the world begins to come back into focus. Assad hears men coughing somewhere in the distance. And for the first time since becoming ill, his senses are alert enough that he can smell the filth all around him, permeating his skin. Slowly he turns his head towards the direction of the voices he has been hearing. His eyes are no longer glazed over and a face starts to come into focus—a young girl. Her arm is extended. She is holding something in her hand. She is smiling. Assad tries to muster the strength to smile back. But then everything slows fades to gray... then turns to black, as more memories begin to emerge.

The port of Beirut is a bustling, crowded stretch of humanity. People shoulder to shoulder, pushing wagons, stacking boxes, shouting out orders. Assad can see a number of ships tied to the dock; all shapes and sizes, some with sails, some without, many relying on the power of coal to propel them across vast oceans. Assad has been told that the man he seeks—Giovanni Galliotti—captains a merchant vessel named the *Il Fiore Del Mare*, which Assad has also been told translates to *The Flower of the Sea*.

Assad walks up and down the busy docks for what seems like hours before setting his sights on a rather large merchant ship tied up at the end of the pier. He sees dozens of men carrying cedar planks up a gangplank while a small, swarthy man wearing a tattered suit coat and clutching a clip board yells out orders at the top of his lungs. Even from this distance Assad can observe the veins on the man's neck bulge, obviously in frustration at something his crew either is or is not doing. Careful not to agitate the man any further, as if that were at all possible, Assad ventures forth to make his presence known. He had been taught some Italian by one of the monks at the monastery who had spent some time in Venice and he was hoping that Galliotti would understand what he was saying.

"Excuse me," Assad says timidly. "Would you be Captain Galliotti?"

"For shit's sake, can't you see I'm busy," he bellows, while at the same time turning to address the person who had approached him. Just as he was about to lash out with another crude observation, the sight of Assad's collar stops him in his tracks. "Oh, sorry, Father, I didn't realize it was you." He quickly and embarrassingly blesses himself. "The abbot said you would be coming on board. We're almost ready to shove off."

"That's quite alright, Captain Galliotti." Assad looks skeptically at the tons of cargo being hoisted onto the ship and the filthy appearance of the crew, many of whom look like they hadn't bathed in weeks. "But, do you usually take on passengers?"

"Usually… no," Galliottti explained. "But every now and then we'll get a few families that are looking to leave this glorious land for one reason or another. And, after all, I *am* a businessman, so if they are able to provide the necessary coin, I try to accommodate them to the best of my abilities." He glances once more at Assad's collar. "It is, after all, the Christian thing to do." Assad was beginning to have his doubts about the man's sincerity. "So just hop on board. Those steps will take you down to the passenger's… quarters. We'll talk soon." And with that Galliotti was off in a flash, barking out more commands at several seemingly disinterested crewmembers leaning against a crate, cigarettes dangling from their lips. One of the men turned and spit on the deck. Assad shuddered with revulsion.

Assad stepped onto the deck and sees the stairs Galliotti had pointed out to him. No sooner is he at the top of the steps then the smell hits him like a physical entity, making his eyes water. He takes out a handkerchief and places it over his nose and mouth as he descends the steps, being careful where he ventures in the dull light. It isn't until he is at the bottom of the stairs that he finds the source of the smell, observing at least 20-25 people—women, children, babies, a few old men—crammed together in an area meant for half that number. Three or four hammocks hang from beams. Dirty cots line the floors. Metal containers are placed discreetly in corners of the ship's hold to capture human waste, some already overflowing. Babies cry and some women whimper in despair. A man—Assad could see his body visibly shaking—vomits into a pail. And this would be their lives—and his life—for the next week or so? It is human despair on a grand scale.

Assad feels like his throat is starting to close up. He gags as his stomach lurches. He covers his mouth tighter with the handkerchief to keep himself from vomiting as he turns and crawls back up the stairs, seeking the fresh air his body so desperately craves. But even that doesn't help as he staggers to the rail and throws up over the side of the ship, the contents of his stomach splashing on to the surface of the water below. After vomiting once more, Assad lays his head down on his hands, waiting for the nausea to pass, his body now drained.

"Maybe you'd feel better, Father, if you had some water to drink," comes a soft voice just off to his left.

Assad slowly raises his head. He sees a young attractive woman, perhaps no more than 30 years old, wearing a long plaid dress, her hair tied up in a bun atop her head. A young girl, perhaps eight years old, sits at her feet, her arm clutching her mother's calf. "Although from the smell I am not sure the water would make you feel any better. Some say it might even make things worse."

"That would be hard to believe," Assad replies, trying his best to smile while the acidy bile does jumping jacks in his stomach. "But I appreciate the information." Assad extends cordially his hand, "My name is Assad Hajjar. It is nice to meet you."

The woman takes Assad's hand. Her grasp is strong but cool. "My name is Johanna Saba. This is my daughter, Anya. It is nice to make your acquaintance." The small child looks up at Assad and smiles. But then her attention is distracted by a fluttering butterfly that had wandered onto the ship, a magnet for the attention of a wide-eyed eight-year old child. She releases her hold on her mother's leg and rises to her feet, her eyes set on capturing the elusive monarch.

"I see you are heading for Italy, also," Johanna said. "Do you have family waiting for you there?" Assad's smile fades. "Sadly, no. Actually, I am leaving my family. But it is my hope that..." Assad never finishes his thought because he is distracted by the horrifying site of Anya balancing herself on the top of the deck's railing, with nothing but a 50-foot drop to an unforgiving sea waiting below her. At the same time, Johanna turns and lets out a scream as she, too, witnesses what is unfolding. Whether it is the suddenness of her mother's scream, or the butterfly fluttering toward open water, Anya suddenly slips and starts falling overboard, as she also lets out a scream of terror. Without even realizing his feet are moving, Assad quickly leaps toward the rail, grabbing it with his left arm as his right arm reaches over the rail, his entire body now off the ground. Miraculously, his right arm is able to grab the collar of Anya's dress, and for a split second she dangles over the open water, until Assad pulls her safely back on deck.

"OWWWW!"

Anya screams with fright as Assad lunges from his soiled cot and grabs Anya's wrist as she tries to bring the cup of water up to his mouth. "Mama! He's hurting me!" she screams, trying to pull her arm away as the cup of water crashes to the floor beside the cot. Assad stares at the girl, unaware of what he is doing, or why she is screaming. But he knows her. Her name is Anya.

Anya's mother slowly takes Assad's arm and gently pries it loose from her daughter. "It's okay, Father," she says soothingly. "Everything is alright. We just wanted to give you some water."

Assad looks at the woman, who is now holding his wrist. She, too, looks familiar. He lies back down on his cot and puts his arm across his eyes. "Where am I?" he asks. Johanna smiles and says," You are on a ship heading for Italy. You have been very sick. I think you might have contracted cholera. But you look better today. I think you may be one of the lucky ones; many aboard the ship have died. You've been in and out of consciousness for the past three days."

It was all coming back to him; the dreams, the memories, they had been real. He looked over at Anya, who was holding her wrist, a tear slowly running down her cheek. "I'm sorry, little one. Did I hurt you?" The girl shakes her head slowly, "No, I'm ok. It doesn't hurt." She smiles bravely.

This time Johanna hands Assad a cup of water, which he gratefully drinks down in one long gulp. "Do you remember now why you are on this ship, and why you are heading to another country?"

Assad sits up, taking a moment to let the tiny slices of pain have their way with him. Once the dance of pain is done, he puts his legs on the floor and sits on the side of the cot. He leans forward, holding his head in his hands.

"Yes," Assad replies. "I remember now why I am going to Rome. It is to start a new life."

Johanna sits on the cot beside him and softly touches his shoulder with her hand. "But what was wrong with your old life?" Assad lifts his head and looks into her eyes. "That life is gone forever. And now, in its place, I must forge a new life…a life in the name of God."

CHAPTER THREE

June 1895

The Port of Messina, Italy

Standing on the bow of the *Il Fiore Del Mare,* Assad marvels at what unfolds before him. The Port of Messina is nestled on the eastern tip of Sicily, just across the strait from the mainland. The port is crowded and noisy, a cacophony of sights and sounds as men scurry about unloading tall-masted ships and small steamers and freighters. Numerous fishing boats are tied up to the dock, men unloading the day's catch, soon to be transported to the local marketplace. A row of three-story stone buildings rim the port, used as housing and retail for various goods. The air is warm and the smell of salt slightly stings Assad's nose.

The week-long journey from Lebanon had been an adventure unto itself, even beyond his contracting of cholera which, thanks be to the Lord, he was able to fight off. Over the days that had passed at sea, Assad had been able to comfort the ship's faithful through a series of priestly endeavors, which included giving last rites to a half-dozen stricken souls, and the delivery and subsequent baptism of one child (another had, sadly, died in childbirth). Assad was even able to conduct Mass, blessing pieces of stale bread to use for communion. He had also wished Johanna and Anya a safe journey, and thanked them for their kindness to him during his time of need. Now, lost in thought and thinking about what the next steps in his journey would entail, thankful for what Italian he had been taught at the Abbey, Assad didn't hear Captain Galliotti come up behind him.

"So Father, what happens from here?" the Captain asked, turning his back slightly from the breeze in order to light his pipe. Over the past few days Assad had come to know Captain Galliotti to some extent. Yes, he was crude, vulgar and occasionally blasphemous, but inside there was a warm glow, one that would every now and then come forward, particularly when speaking of his daughter, Frances Ersillia, whom he lovingly called *Mia Piccola Rosa* (My Little Rose).

"I guess I'll be heading to Rome, to the Vatican," Assad softly replied. "I have a letter of introduction from Father Abbot to one of the priests there."

"I'm sure Rome can always use another priest," Galliotti answers. "You can't throw a rock in Rome without hitting clergy of some type." Assad smiles. "That's probably true. What do you suggest as the best means of transport?"

Galliotti pondered the question. "Well, you could do horse and carriage, but the trip would be extremely long and very uncomfortable. My opinion, it is best to travel by rail. There are trains in Messina that go directly into *Stazione Termini* in Rome. That is what I would do if I…"

"POPPA!"

Galliotti never finished the thought as he turned to greet a child, perhaps 14 or 15, running up the gangplank, her ponytail flying in the breeze, dress fluttering. No more than a few feet from Galliotti, she leaped into his arms with a laugh, hugging him hard, forcing him to stagger back a few steps. "I missed you!" she squeals.

The look on the Captain's gruff face, now beaming with delight, said it all; this was his *Piccola Rosa*. Assad smiled at the warm reunion.

"It's great to see you, too, little one. How are Momma and your sisters?" he asked gently setting her down on the deck. "They are all fine," she replied. "And your brother?" Galliotti inquired. Assad couldn't help but notice at the mention of her brother that the girl suddenly withdrew into herself. It wasn't overly obvious, but Assad could see she was troubled by the question. "He is ok," she said, averting her eyes slightly, her left hand unconsciously scratching at her right forearm, where Assad could see there was already a series of fingernail marks from previous scratching. Assad took it to be a nervous habit.

"Good, good," the Captain responded "Here, I want you to meet someone." Galliotti placed his hands lightly on his daughter's shoulders and turned her slightly in Assad's direction. "This is Father Assad. Father, this is my daughter, Frances Ersillia Galliotti. *Mia Piccola Rosa.*"

"It is very nice to meet you, Frances," Assad said with a slight bow. "Your father has spoken of you often on this journey. But I see now meeting you in person that his description of you as being beautiful was simply modesty on his part." Frances blushed at the comments from an obviously older, but very handsome stranger. "It is nice to meet you as well, Father." She replied with a small curtsey.

Galliotti spoke up. "Father Assad is on his way to Rome, where he'll be meeting The Pope!"

"Well, I am not sure I'll actually get to…"

"You're going to meet Pope Leo XIII!" Frances exclaimed excitedly, her eyes now as wide as saucers. "That's like meeting... God!"

"Well," Assad chuckled. "Close, but not quite. I hope I have the opportunity, though."

But Frances could not contain her excitement. "You *must* write to me when you meet him... tell me what he is like. Will you promise to do that—Poppa—give Father our address so he can write to me! Hurry!!"

"Okay, okay, be patient," her father replied, fishing a crumpled business card out of his inside pocket. "Here you go Father. The address is here. I am sure it would make a little girl happy."

"It would be my pleasure, Captain Galliotti. But now I must be off. I am sure it will be a long journey." He shakes the man's hand and once again bows graciously in Frances' direction. "And I hope I will see you again soon, young lady." She blushes once again, "Have a safe trip, Father." Then almost as an afterthought she blurts out to Assad as he walks down the plank and onto the dock... "And don't forget to write me!"

CHAPTER FOUR

June 1895

Stazione Termini, Rome, Italy

The train trip had been long, but thanks to the Captain's good advice it was not duly uncomfortable. Assad had even made time to chat with several of the passengers seated around him. He met a young woman with two small children traveling to visit her sister; a young man, obviously very nervous, on his way to Naples to propose to a girl he had only met through correspondence; and a middle-aged gentleman, who turned out to be a laborer, his hands strong and heavily-calloused, and who was being drawn to Rome by the promise of work as the city begins to industrialize.

As Assad departs the train and makes his way into the terminal, the thick crowd buzzes as loud conversations slips in and out of one another, with seemingly everyone heading in different locations. Finally making his way to an exit and on to the sidewalk, Assad once again is met with a sense of wonder at a world far removed from his tiny village of Altou. On each side of the street Assad has to look up at towering buildings, some seven or eight floors high, sidewalks lined with gas lamps and trees showing off buds just starting to awaken in the warm spring sunshine. Assad sees men with mustaches dressed in dark suits with ties and high-collars, women in long-flowing dresses and collars up to their chins, quickly navigating the crossing of streets while horse-drawn buggies travel to and fro at a rapid pace over the cobblestones that make up Rome's streets. Assad's head swirls at the myriad of movement all around him as he stood on the sidewalk, his battered suitcase in his hand, drinking in the activity unfolding in this great city so far from home. A voice brought him back.

"Excuse me, Father, would you be needing a ride someplace?"

Assad turns to his right to see a young man with a cap and a large drooping mustache, sitting atop his buggy, his grey horse seemingly oblivious to the question being posed while perfectly content instead to chew on the remnants of a carrot. "I'm sorry," Assad answers. "Did you say something?"

"I said do you need a ride? Is there someplace I can take you?"

Assad steps forward and puts his bag in the back of the buggy. "Yes, please, Vatican City, if you would?" He makes himself comfortable in the back seat, still looking at the humanity around him. "Right away," the driver replies, prompting the horse to move forward, the carrot long devoured.

As he travels along the streets, Assad is amazed at the contradiction of seeing lavish buildings sprouting from the streets, but a mere few blocks away the buildings are only half-built, the construction now put on hold for no apparent reason. All around the building he can see ramshackle shacks, with people sitting outside, using open fires to heat whatever is in the contents of large black pots. It is a sad and depressing sight. The driver somehow senses Assad's dismay.

"Looks pretty bad, don't it, Father?" The driver says. "The city has been doing a lot of building the last few years but there are areas that seem to get more attention than others, often depending on who is living there, like politicians, rich merchants, and so on." He drives a few more blocks then continues. "This neighborhood is called Testaccio, and it's pretty bad off, which I am sure you can see. I'm told there are maybe 10,000 or more families crammed into this one area, very often with entire families living in not more than two or three rooms; no water, no gas, no way to keep clean. It's awful. God help them."

Assad can only shake his head at the misery as the carriage continues through the streets, carving a swath through the human despair.

Twenty minutes later Assad can see Vatican City looming up in front of him, sending a tingle through his spine; could any Christian not react at such a sight? Now entering St. Peter's Square, the open space which lies in front of the basilica, Assad recalls reading how it was designed in the mid-17th century so that the greatest number of people could see the Pope give his blessing, either from the middle of the façade of the church or from a window in the Vatican Palace. In the center of the square lay a massive obelisk and a granite fountain. Massive columns flank both the left and right sides of the basilica, fanning out like maternal arms, engulfing the faithful. It is truly a splendid sight to behold, with people and carriages moving about in all directions.

"I believe the priests' quarters are in the back, off the courtyard," Assad's driver offers. "I'll take you around."

"No, that's fine, my son," Assad answers, fishing several coins out of his pocket. He hands them to the driver and grabs his bag. "I think I'd like to walk over." The driver thanks him, tips his cap, and drives off, leaving Father Assad Hajjar standing in the middle of the holiest place in Rome.

Almost self-consciously patting the letter of introduction tucked inside his coat pocket, written by Father Abbot, Assad ventures forth towards the courtyard. He knows from reading the letter whom he is supposed to meet. Passing through the courtyard, Assad observes several priests sitting about on benches, many reading the Bible or fingering rosary beads, heads bowed in silent prayer. Approaching the large wooden doors that he assumes is the entrance to the priest's quarter; Assad uses the large metal knockers to announce his arrival. After several minutes, the doors open wide.

"Yes, can I help you?"

Assad assesses the old priest standing in front him, one hand on the door. He is perhaps 60 years old or better, extremely thin, his shoulders arched and his chin pushed down towards his chest, giving him an almost bird-like appearance. Assad answers, "I am Father Assad, from Lebanon." He holds out the letter of introduction, which will further explain his presence.

41

The old priest does not move. Suddenly, Assad feels ashamed, not because he is standing their looking silly holding out a letter, but because he failed to realize the priest is blind. "I'm sorry," he sputters. "I have a letter of introduction. I didn't realize...."

"No need to explain Father Assad from Lebanon," the priest quickly answers, but not without a small smile curling up the side of his lip. "I am sure it is an outstanding letter, and very well-written. Why don't you tell me who it says you wish to see and we'll begin from there?"

Scanning the letter in order to make sure there is no mistake, Assad says, "I am to be received by... Father Pietro D'Angelo."

"Ahh, Father Pietro," repeats the priest." A fine man of God. Please come this way. I'll take you to him."

As the old priest leads Assad through the foyer, down a long hallway and up a flight of stairs, he can't help but be impressed by how the blind priest easily navigates the route, never once bumping into a chair, a wall, or a table. Assad assumes he had navigated the same course hundreds of times and now it was permanently ingrained in his senses. But still, very impressive. When they finally came to a wooden door, the priest knocks loudly, "Father Pietro, you have a visitor who has traveled many miles to meet with you." From beyond the closed door came a low rumbling voice: "Come in, Father Assad. I've been anxiously awaiting your visit." The priest opens the door and beckons Assad to enter the room. Once Assad steps into the room the blind priest closes the door. Assad can barely make out the sound of his sandals scurrying down the hallway as he looks back at the door. He then turns to face his host.

Struggling slightly to lift his sizeable girth from his chair—Father Pietro is easily over 300 pounds—he comes out from behind the desk, his hand outstretched, which Assad takes with a smile on his face, only to have it fade as his hand is tightly squeezed under the considerable strength of Father Pietro's massive right hand.

"So very nice to finally meet you... how was your trip? Long and tiring I assume? Please sit," he says, waving him to a chair in front of the desk. Assad does as he is instructed, while at the same time passing the letter to the portly priest who has returned to his chair. He takes a second to scrutinize its contents, his lips moving ever so slightly, his voice barely audible, as he reads what Father Abbot has written. "Yes, I see... hmmm... good, good." He looks up at Assad, smiles and folds the letter, placing it in the top draw of the scarred, wooden desk. Assad is slightly little taken aback that the letter is not returned to him, but chooses not to press the point at this time.

"So, Father Assad from Lebanon…" The rotund priest leans forward on to the desk, his wide red face beaming. "What shall we do with you?"

"If it pleases you, Father Pietro," Assad replies, "I'd like to make a suggestion."

CHAPTER FIVE

July 1896

Testaccio, Italy

Rome's July sun is unrelenting, pounding on Assad like a sledgehammer as he helps serve food outdoors to many of the families living in Testaccio, perhaps the worst slums in Italy. Several years ago the intent here was to build housing to shelter Rome's growing population. The plan called for 36 buildings to be constructed. But by the summer of 1896, only nine had been completed, and another six only partially built. This meant that nearly 8,000 people had to suffer the direst living conditions; no gas, no water, human waste being dumped in empty lots, streets left unpaved. It was an area ripe for the festering of disease, resulting in one of every two children dying before they can even celebrate their sixth birthday. Assad had visited ramshackle dwellings offering prayer and hope, only to witness as many as five people living in a single room. The heartbreak was immense.

As he spooned some soup into the cracked pottery cup of an old woman, Assad couldn't help but smile while recalling the look on the pudgy face of Father Pietro when he asked him over a year ago what he intended to do. The portly priest was stunned, "Why on earth would you want to undertake such a sorrowful mission?" he had asked shaking his head. "It is an area ripe with death and desolation."

Assad never hesitated with his answer, "That is the very reason I *must* do this," Assad earnestly replied. "God has given me a second chance, the opportunity to be here today, in his majestic house. It is important that I pay Him back such an honor in any way I can. And also, I made a promise to my father."

Sitting in his humble apartment this evening, Assad is exhausted from the day's events. Aside from helping at the food distribution center, he had also helped build a wall in a building to separate several families forced to live together, plus gave last rites to three men, a woman, and, tragically, a two-year old. He also found the opportunity, as the area had no church, to say mass, using a wooden door placed on two large stones as an altar.

Assad was fortunate to have an apartment all to himself. It was small but comfortable, with a separate room off a kitchen. He felt guilty living in this "opulence," but the residents of Testaccio had insisted on it. They have come over the past year to see him as more than just a priest, but as someone who they could depend on, look to, seek advice from, at any time of the day or night. It was as if in all the despair that loomed large around them each and every day would be made tolerable, because in Assad they saw that beacon of light. And thus, they had banded together to make sure that beacon never flamed out, only to leave them once again in darkness.

Sitting now at a wooden table in his kitchen, as summer slipped into autumn, the light from a kerosene lamp providing the only illumination, Assad sat and began to compose a letter he had been meaning to write for months. As he started to place pen to paper, he briefly glanced at the crumpled business card on the table, a card he had carried with him on his long journey from the Port of Messina just over a year ago.

October 10, 1896

To: Miss Frances Ersillia Galliotti
Fr: Father Assad Hajjar

Dear Miss Frances,

I hope this letter finds you well.

Alas, I have yet to meet His Holiness, but hope to soon. And I am sure when I do I will have grand stories to tell about that meeting.

In the meantime, I am doing God's work in an area of Rome known as Testaccio. Oh, Miss Frances, I wish you could see it and the despair that many people are forced to endure on a daily basis. They have such hardships that they must overcome each and every day. There is a lack of food, water, medicine, the many elements that many of us take for granted, because they are either parts of our daily lives or easily accessible. But here, it is not so. I try to help them the best I can, offering spiritual guidance and physical labor, both in the name of helping to ease their daily suffering. But, sadly, I am only one man.

But what I find remarkable, Miss Frances, is the spirit of these people. Who continue to struggle each day but also take the opportunity to smile and be grateful for what meager gifts are bestowed on them. Their hearts are large and their sense of caring deep. They are certainly God's children.

But enough about my daily trials and tribulations; How are you? Have you had any exciting adventures? I hope you will write me back as I am sure receiving a letter from you would brighten my day.

I wish you the best and hope you will give the same to Captain Galliotti.

Yours in prayer,

Assad

A return letter came soon after.

January 27, 1897

To: Father Assad Hajjar
Fr: Frances Ersillia Galliotti

Dear Father,

How wonderful to hear from you! I am sure that Rome is a wondrous place, with huge statues, lavish fountains, crowded shopping areas, and, of course, The Vatican. How I long to someday see it.

I was saddened to hear about the conditions in Testaccio—oh, those poor people! And the children! Do they have schools there? You are so kind to devote your time, and your life, to helping them. You are truly doing God's work.

By comparison, my life isn't as exciting as your, but you did ask about adventures. It's not very big but I am working in an office for a local politician where we live. I believe he is a good man, but for some reason Poppa doesn't approve of him. And that makes me angry. He still treats me like a child, although I know deep down he feels like he is protecting me. I do love him so.

I will write to you again soon.

Cordially, Frances

The letter, written at least a month ago made Assad smile.

"Father, please come. Quick!"

Assad looks up quickly from Frances' letter to see a small girl, perhaps no more than eight or nine, standing in his doorway, her dress ragged and torn, her cheeked smudged with dirt. She could have easily been one of a thousand such children buried beneath the rubble of the poverty all around her.

"What is it, my child?"

"Dr. Santini needs you. He says we are losing another one."

Dr. Gino Santini was a great man. He was a very well respected physician at Rome Hospital who was now devoting some of his time to helping the poor of Testaccio. Assad knew the frustration that Dr. Santini felt, having to work in squalid conditions, with poor lighting and little or no sanitation. But he was relentless in his commitment to doing whatever he could.

Assad and the child quickly left the apartment and walked the several blocks to a first-level apartment that had been crudely fashioned as a clinic. Upon entering he saw the doctor only from the back, hovering over a patient, his breath laboring as he looked down at a small boy lying on a makeshift operating table, moaning.

"Is that you, Assad?"

"Yes, Doctor. I am here."

"Good. Send the child away. I need you."

Assad bent down and gave the girl a small piece of candy he had in his pocket. "Thank you, child. Now run along." The child glanced over at Dr. Santini, then up at Assad. Apparently satisfied that she had completed her mission, she smiled and ran off.

"Now, Assad!"

The priest hurried over to Dr. Santini's side. What he saw forced him to take a step back. The boy lying on the table couldn't have been much older than the girl who fetched him.

He was lying on the table moaning, his eyes closed and head lolling from one side to another. Even without feeling the boy's brow, Assad could tell he was on fire. But what caught Assad's eye the most was the boy's left leg. From the knee down the leg was swollen and an ugly shade of purple and green. And poised over the knee was a wicked-looking saw being wielded by a red-faced Dr. Santini.

"I need you to hold him down, Assad. I gave him some Laudanum but it's not going to completely knock him out."

"What happened to his leg? And where are his parents? Where is his mother?"

"As for the leg, my best guess is he cut it on some scrap metal and it got infected. They sell the scrap to help feed their family. I need to remove this leg before the fever and infection kill him. As for the second part of your question... *who the hell knows?* A stranger found him lying in the road. Christ, what I wouldn't give for a decent place to work! Now stop asking questions and hold him down!"

Assad places his hands gently on the boy's shoulders, but with enough pressure to pin him to the table. But when the doctor's blade starts to cut through skin with a sickening sound, the boy's entire upper body arches with such conviction that a stunned Assad has to increase his pressure. Before Dr. Santini could cut further, the boy let out a last gasp, his body shuddered twice, then went still. The cutting stopped, the room fell quiet. Dr. Santini put down his saw. He looked at the boy with a deep sadness etched on his face as Father Assad administered last rites. Dr. Santini sat down heavily on a soiled chair and put his heads in his hands. "Assad, we are going to keep losing these people without a proper medical facility," he said slowly. "Something has to happen...soon."

"I know," says Assad, putting a sheet over the prone child. "But where would we get money for something like that? You see how these people live."

"How much money would you need?"

Dr. Santini looks up to observe the source of the question, which was posed by a young woman standing in the doorway, a small suitcase clutched in her hand. "My father has money. Lots of money"

"And who exactly are you, young lady, if I may ask?"

Father Assad took the liberty of answering. "Dr. Gino Santini, I have the honor of presenting Miss Frances Ersillia Galliotti, from Messina. And I have no idea why she is here."

Once again sitting at the table in his apartment, this time with Frances sitting across from him clutching a cup of tea, Frances explained the circumstances that brought her to Rome. Her first stop had been the Vatican, where she learned Assad was living and doing God's work in Testaccio. And it was fortunate that the first person she asked of his whereabouts was the young girl who had just exited the building. The rest of the circumstances that brought her to his kitchen were just as enlightening.

"You recall I wrote you about that politician I was working with in my last letter?" Assad nodded. "Well, part of the job involved that I would need to travel to various locations to assist him, sometimes overnight… but nothing ever happened, I swear," she quickly offers. "But Poppa said I was shameful and a disgrace to the family and told me I had to leave the house." She slowly takes a sip of her tea. "I didn't know where to go; I have no real friends. One of our servants suggested the Catholic Church in Rome might take me in. And that's when I remembered our letters, and that's why I was looking for you." She looked up at Assad. "You must think me horrible. I should never have come." She put the cup down and started to rise from the chair.

"No, I am glad you did," Assad says softly, taking her hands in his. She sits back down.

"You can stay here, use the bedroom. I can sleep on one of the overstuffed chairs out here.   It will be fine." He smiled. "Besides, as you saw, we can really use an extra pair of hands."

Frances blushed. "But what would people say, what would people think?"

"They will think you have been sent by God because of the good work you will do... and they will embrace you as they have me." She smiles. "So tell me, Frances Ersillia Galliotti, now that you have seen firsthand the task that we face in these sad surroundings, what would *you* like to do?"

Frances barely hesitated before answering, "I want to teach the children. And a teacher needs a school." She takes a sheet of paper and a pen from her valise and puts them down on the table. Assad was stunned by the determination in her eyes. "I know my father feels I let him down, but I truly believe he still loves me dearly. And I also truly believe that he is a good man and when he hears about what we are facing he will muster the needed resources to provide Testaccio with the clinic and schoolroom it so desperately needs. Now I have a letter to write... so please make me another cup of tea."

Assad smiles as he rises from his chair and looks slightly awestruck at what he is witnessing. But all he could say as he walks over to the stove is, "Yes, ma'am."

The summer of 1897 had been eventful in a number of ways. First, to Assad's surprise but not Frances', Captain Galliotti had consented to funding the building of a small clinic, under the supervision of Dr. Santini, and, to the delight of his daughter, a classroom and supplies to benefit 25-30 children at a time. The Captain initially balked, but inevitably relented to Father Assad's conviction that both the clinic and the school bear his name.

The other event that unfolded that summer was even more profound. Though in Assad's heart, he would admit he wasn't totally shocked. Frances was pregnant.

Despite their desire to keep their relationship platonic; she in the bedroom and he on the chair in the other room. Their proximity and the love they were feeling for each other caused the space between them to close in, as if the very apartment itself had started to shrink. It all culminated in a soft and touching evening in May. Frances was beside herself when she gave the news to Assad about her condition. "Oh, Assad, what shall we do? You're a priest. You'll be banished from the order when the Vatican hears this!"

Assad thought long and hard about the situation and eventually came to some decisions. He could leave the priesthood but still remain a priest. However, that would not be possible if he married. Therefore, he would just have Frances take his name—Frances Hajjar—and everyone would assume they were married, even if it were not so.

"Oh, Assad, are you sure that's what you want to do", she asked him, her eyes brimming with tears. "It is too much of a sacrifice to make." He smiled. "It will all be fine; I'll still be a priest, albeit with certain... limitations. I will still be able to do His work for the people of Testaccio. I will travel to Rome tomorrow and meet with Father Pietro, to tell him of my decision. It will be fine... you'll see. He will completely understand my decision."

"No, I *don't* understand your decision!" Father Pietro's ample face was crimson and beads of sweat popped on his brow. "Let me understand this, you want to leave the priesthood... is that correct?"

"It is Father."

"But still perform some of your priestly duties for the good and deserving people of Testaccio? Do you want to tell me what brings you to this momentous decision?"

Assad thought a moment about the question being posed, then replied, "I'd rather not. But I understand from everything I have read that I have the right to ask for this request, is that not true, Father?"

Father Pietro hoisted his immense body from the chair and stalked his small office, his arms waving wildly. "Yes, of course you do. I just want to make sure you understand the full ramifications and consequences of what you are asking. And if not, let me explain them to you."

Father Pietro went over to a small bookcase and after a brief scrutiny of what was available to him, pulled out a thick, leather bound book. Putting on his glasses he proceeded to flip through the pages until he found the one he wanted. "Now listen, Assad, so that you *do* understand." He cleared his throat and read aloud.

"When a man is ordained as a priest, he receives this sacred character to act in the person of Christ and as His instrument for His Church. He also receives faculties from the Bishop of the Diocese or other legitimate authority to perform His ministry."

"Are you with me so far, Father Assad?" Assad nodded. "Good, because now we come to the part about what happens when a priest leaves the priesthood?" Father Pietro looked back down at the pages and continued.

"Since Holy Orders is a character sacrament, once it has been validly received, it never is invalidated for any reason whatsoever. A priest may be freed from the clerical state and dispensed from the promise of celibacy..." Assad almost found himself smiling at that but wisely held his composure. "... by the proper authority. He may no longer have the obligations or the privileges to function as a cleric, but nevertheless he remains a cleric. Commonly, this practice is called *laicization*, meaning 'returned to the state of the laity,' as highlighted in the *Code of Canon Law*, #290-293. Even though the cleric has been laicized and no longer functions as a priest he still has the sacramental character of Holy Orders. Technically, if he were to perform a sacrament in accord with the norms of the Church, that sacrament would indeed be valid. However—are you listening Assad?-- the sacrament would be *illicit*, meaning he violated Church law and would be culpable for this infraction since he no longer has the faculties to function as a priest."

Father Pietro slammed the book shut, more for dramatic effect than anything else. "Well?"

Assad answered slowly, "But if I am to understand the full extent of what we are discussing, it's that the *Code of Canon Law* makes one exception for emergency circumstances. I believe I read, 'Even though he lacks the faculty to hear confession, any priest validly and licitly absolves from any kind of censures and sins any penitent who is in danger of death, even if an approved priest is present.' I believe that means the Church is recognizing the indelible spiritual character received by the priest– although now laicized– at his ordination." Father Pietro started to speak but Assad stopped him by holding up his hand. "Please Father, if I may continue." Father Pietro let loose a defeated sigh and reluctantly nodded. "For instance, suppose a person was hurt in an accident, maybe run over by a wagon and was dying. And no priest could be found to hear the person's confession. A laicized priest– maybe having not functioned as a priest for years– could licitly hear a dying person's confession and validly absolve him from all sin." Father Assad sat back in his chair, his hands clasped in his lap. "At least, that is what I read."

Father Pietro simply put his head down on his desk, and without looking up said, "Okay Assad, you win. I will put the proper paperwork through the Vatican office. Now do me a favor." Assad rose from his chair. "Of course, Father Pietro, what is it you wish of me?" Father Pietro simply lifted his right arm and pointed to the door. "Get out of my office." Assad smiled and left.

The summer and fall of 1897 had been a happy time for Assad and Frances. The baby was due in February and it was decided on what the name would be; Khalil if a boy, Inez if a girl The area that would house the schoolroom was beginning to be worked on by Captain Galliotti's men (and of course his considerable resources) and the work on the clinic would commence in the spring. The good Captain, however, had no idea he was about to become a grandfather. It was Frances' idea to withhold that information until after the baby was born. Assad agreed, albeit reluctantly, although a part of him was reluctant to see the look on the Captain's face when he realized who the father was.

While the schoolroom was under construction, Frances happily did the teaching in their humble apartment, which quickly became quite crowded. The children, all sitting cross-legged on the floor, loved her and her enthusiasm was infectious. But, alas, even happy times very often have a time limit.

"Assad! Something is wrong. I can feel it!"

The bed is soaked from the sweat of Frances' body as she writhes in pain, her hands over her swollen belly. The large woman positions herself at the foot of the bed. Her apron is spotted with some of Frances' blood. She is a midwife, one that had delivered well over 20 babies in Testaccio. But the look of concern on her face offered Assad no comfort. He silently began to pray.

"Push, Frances… you must push!" she says in a soothing voice.

Frances' body arches as she does what the midwife has instructed. She let out a cry. Assad puts a cloth on her forehead. "Almost there… *PUSH!*"

This time her cry is louder, more intense. But she musters her strength to push with what strength she has left.

"That's it, that's it… okay. You can relax now. It's a girl."

The midwife holds the unmoving child in her arms and places it gently in a basket. She slaps the baby lightly on its backside. Nothing. Then again. Nothing.

Frances grabs Assad's hand tightly and looks up at him with questioning eyes. "Assad, why is the baby not crying? What is wrong?"

"I... I don't know, my love." He looks at the midwife, hoping for an answer. But he can tell by the look on her face the answer is not something he, nor Frances, would want to hear."

"I'm sorry, Father."

Upon hearing the words, Frances lets out a painful wail, her head rocking from side to side. He tries to embrace her but she pushes him away. "My beautiful baby! My beautiful Inez!!" And as the wailing continues, Assad has never felt more helpless.

March 5, 1898

To: Captain Giovanni Galliotti, Port of Messina
Fr: Father Assad Hajjar

Dear Captain Galliotti,

I hope this letter finds you in good health.

I write to you today as a man full of thanks and despair. The gratitude I feel for what you have undertaken to help these poor people of Testaccio can never be fully conveyed. Once finished, the clinic and the school will enhance their lives in a most positive way. What you are doing will not go unnoticed by He who is all-knowing.

But, alas, I also carry a deep depression, one which I must share with you. It's about Frances.

As you are well aware from her letter to you about the conditions in Testaccio, she has been staying here. She had nowhere to stay after her dispute with you so I did what I felt was the Christian thing to do and gave her a spare room in my apartment. She took to the people of Testaccio almost immediately, particularly the children as she displayed a knack to teach, hence her requesting funds from you to construct a schoolroom.

But the remainder of the reason for my letter to you is also one of embarrassment, though in my heart that is the wrong word to use. As I need not tell you, your daughter, Frances, is a beautiful woman; strong-willed with an independent streak. And I found myself falling in love with her, a feeling so strong and overpowering that even religion could not keep us apart. Last summer she informed me she was pregnant with our child.

I know how you must feel about me, a man of the cloth. But you should also know that upon hearing the news I immediately went to the Vatican and asked to leave the priesthood, which they granted. If there is forgiveness to be given, I hope you will give it, both to myself and, most importantly, to your daughter.

Alas, there is sadness. Due to some complications, this past winter our child—a girl—failed to survive childbirth. Your granddaughter. It is not uncommon in these conditions. It is a sad fact of life in Testaccio. And since it has happened, Frances has gone into a deep depression. She will not eat; she does not leave the apartment. The children come to our home day after day to be taught but she will not see them. I feel she also feels guilty that the child was the reason behind my leaving the priesthood and she failed me... failed God. But nothing could be further from the truth.

Captain Galliotti, I implore you to visit. Frances needs you desperately. Please come.

Yours in God,
Father Assad Hajjar

"Frances, you must eat something," Assad urges. "You are losing much too much weight. It will make you feel better." Frances, sitting at the table, slumped in her chair, pushes the bowl away from in front of her. "I am not hungry." She looks up at Assad. Her face and eyes had been red for days, a result of what seemed like daily bouts of crying. "Will food bring back Inez... will food bring back your religious vows that I took from you?" She starts to sob again.

"I told you, you are not to...." A knock at the door. "Please come back later," Assad shouts without turning from Frances. Another knock. Frustrated, Assad rises from his chair and walks to the door. He opens it quickly, "I said, would you please..." He does not finish his thought.

Captain Giovanni Galliotti's imposing figure fills the doorway. Assad does not know what to say. He could tell his mouth was hanging open and quickly closed it. The man looked at Assad, but here was no hate in his eyes.

"Can I still call you Father Assad?" Not knowing what to say, Assad nods dumbly.

Captain Galliotti steps a few feet into the apartment and looks at his daughter as she rise slowly from the table. "Poppa?"

"I am here *Mia Piccola Rosa*. Poppa is here."

Frances slowly walks over to her father and they tightly embrace.

"Poppa, I am so sorry. I wanted to wait to tell you after Inez was born. I wanted you to be proud of me. I failed you so much." She sobs into his chest.

"Shhh, it's alright child. You did no such thing. Poppa is very proud of you. Assad told me of the wonderful work you do here, and the great sacrifice he made for you. I could not be prouder... for both of you." Galliotti looks at Assad, who simply nods in gratitude.

"Things will be alright, Frances. You will see." He holds his daughter at arm's length and smiles at her. "Now get your Poppa a cup of coffee. It's been a long journey. Then we will talk some more."

CHAPTER SIX

Christmas Eve, 1908
Messina, Italy

"Poppa, help me hang the ornament on the tree. I can't reach!"

"Hold on a minute, Khalil," Assad says to his eight-year-old son. "I'll be right there."

Ten years had swiftly passed since the day Captain Galliotti came to his door to comfort Frances. But for Assad, that visit was like a beacon of light in that it led to his Frances finding her way out of the deep dark tunnel of depression she had fallen into after the death at childbirth of Inez.

"Poppa, how come Khalil gets to hang things but I can't? The question is asked by a very determined six-year old, her arms crossed and a scowl on her beautiful face. "Don't worry, little one… you'll get your chance," Assad answers in his most diplomatic voice. But he knew in his heart that asking Tecla to be patient was akin to asking a fish not to swim or a rooster not to crow. Khalil sticking his tongue out at his younger sister does nothing to defuse the situation.

Assad sits in a large comfortable chair in the living room of Captain Galliotti's lavish home in Messina and surveys the events unfolding around him. The room, which is almost as big as Assad's entire apartment in Testacchio, is filled with joy and excitement as several neighbors and some of the servants help decorate the tree, bringing with them various desserts and other goodies. Assad turns his attention back to the notebook in his lap. He labors in writing the sermon for the Christmas Day Mass as his attention is constantly distracted by the movement about him. Although he had officially left the priesthood many years ago (much to the dismay of Father Pietro), he was still performing masses for the residents of Testaccio. It still brought him a level of joy and comfort. And now he had been asked to do a reading at the Cathedral of the Assumption in Messina, by no less than the Archbishop of Messina himself, Letterio D'Arrigo Ramondini.

"You know, you are never going to finish that sermon until you finish that tree."

Assad looks up into the smiling face of his beloved Frances, holding three-year-old Inez, named after the child she had lost, snugly in her arms. The small child purrs on her chest, hovering somewhere between sleep and awake. Assad smiles—he knew she was right. But a certain level of contentment, mixed with equal portions of satisfaction and gratitude, keeps him rooted in his chair, taking in all around him.

In the little over 10 years that had passed since Assad made the decision to do God's work within the slums of Testaccio, so much had happened. Aside from the joy of seeing his three children born, the continued upgrading of the neighborhood had been nothing short of remarkable. What had once been deemed a horrible ghetto, rife with disease and poverty due to the horrendous overcrowding and high mortality rate among its young people, Testaccio had now turned the corner. Although certainly nothing along the scales of Rome, or even Naples, Assad could see a definite pride in ownership among its residents. Streets were cleaner and flowers were starting to bloom in places you would never think possible a decade ago. And much of what had been accomplished thus far had been directly the result of Frances father.

Honoring his commitment' to help the people of Testaccio, Captain Galliotti had poured considerable resources into the neighborhood. The fall of 1904 saw the opening of Testaccio's first school, with the Captain also furnishing books, paper, pencils, and writing tablets. Frances taught the children there each day, for at least four hours per day. There was no shortage of babysitters for the children among the grateful mothers who now had the opportunity to see their children earn an education.

The next philanthropic shoe to drop, so to speak, came in the shape of the Galliotti Clinic, a much needed facility where doctors from Rome, Naples and as far away as Messina, could spend a set number of hours per day tending to the sick and afflicted. It was not uncommon to see people lined up on the sidewalk outside waiting to be treated. It was also not unusual for Assad to spend several hours a day at the clinic, offering comfort to those in need.

As Testaccio started to bloom, commerce started to take notice. More and more stores started to open up; a butcher shop, clothing store, a small storefront that specialized in children's toys and games, even a dentist. Also taking notice were trade unions that started the neighborhood some 10 years ago and now have seen enough growth to commence what they had started as more and more buildings were completed, offering more suitable housing with less over-crowding.

Assad's thoughts were interrupted by a booming voice coming from the next room, "Ho-Ho-Ho… who wants presents!"

"Grand-poppa!" both Khalil and Tecla screamed in unison. Captain Galliotti enters the room only to be greeted by the onslaught of two excited children latching on to him. He carries a large bag, as do several men behind him. Assad knows them to be the men who worked on the building of the clinic.

"*Ooomph!* You're going to knock your poor old Grand-poppa over," he exclaims, a broad smile spreading across his ruddy features. Assad knows how much the Captain has come to cherish these moments, which was one of the main reasons he and Frances had agreed to spend this Christmas with him.

The two men put the bags on the floor, doffed their caps in Frances' direction, and silently leave the room. Captain Galliotti does likewise with his bag, while at the same time stopping two sets of eager hands from trying to open them.

"Uh-uh, these are not to be opened until tomorrow morning," the Captain explains. "Which means the quicker you are in bed tonight, the quicker the morning will come and the sooner *La Befana* will arrive." The look on both Khalil and Tecla's face was one of disappointment and sadness. But the Captain quickly solves the problem as he reaches into his inside coat pocket.

"But until then, perhaps these will help you wait?"

The children's faces light up as their Grand-poppa pulls out two large lollipops—the largest lollipops Assad had ever seen— and hands them to Khalil and Tecla. He then turns to Inez, still buried in her mother's arms but taking in everything that is unfolding in front of her. "And for my littlest one, I have this." And at that he hands her a small doll. The child hesitates, but only slightly, before grabbing the doll and hugging it to her chest. He kisses the child softly on her head. "You look just like my Marie," says the Captain, remembering his wife who passed many years ago when Frances was still a child.

"Poppa, you spoil the children," Frances says, the words seeming to catch in her throat.

"I know," he said. "But that's what Grand-poppa's are supposed to do."

The room is quiet, lit only by the glow from the fireplace. Assad looks at his watch… 9:50pm. It was two days after Christmas and it seemed like only now, what with the whirlwind of excitement that seemed to blow around him like a small typhoon, that Assad could pause and reflect on what had transpired. Sitting on the couch with Frances leaning on him, her breathing soft, Assad thanks God for all He had bestowed on him these last few days. Christmas morning unfolded splendidly. The children were thrilled with their presents and his sermon was well-received by the congregation.

The plan was to board a train tomorrow, December 28, for the journey back to Rome. From there they would catch a ride to Testaccio. Assad knew Frances missed the children from her classrooms and longed to return to her duties there. Their traveling bags and luggage sat just inside the front door in preparation for an early morning departure. The big house was quiet, empty except for his family, Captain Galliotti and several servants who live-in.

Frances snuggled closer but did not awake. He knew they should turn in as they faced a long ride back to Rome. Not wanting to wake her when he stood, Assad bent down, and uses his arms to lift her gently into his. He starts to walk up the stairs to where the bedrooms are.

"Assad, I am happy," she murmurs, not quite awake. "Are you happy?"

"Yes, my love… very happy."

"I am glad."

He continues his journey up the staircase.

Assad was on a boat, a boat being tossed mercilessly by a raging ocean. He could hear the masts cracking and breaking apart, people screaming, windows shattering, as on his bed, which was now moving across the room like some carnival ride, began to fall apart. He was tossed from the bed by the violent motion, hitting the floor hard, his head banging on the wood. Then, darkness.

"ASSAD! WAKE UP!

Frances' frantic voice starts to bring him back. He is somehow on the floor of their bedroom. He tries to shake away the cobwebs that clutter his brain, making it hard for him to comprehend what is happening. But this he did know—their room was breaking apart. *Earthquake*!

Assad manages to get to his feet, his head still woozy from where it struck the floor. Looking through a bedroom window that was no longer there, Assad could see it is barely dawn, likely not much after 5:00am. The room shifts again and pictures fly from the wall.

"WHERE ARE THE CHILDREN?" he cries out. Assad grabs Frances by her arms and brings her to her feet. She seems in a state of shock. "FRANCES!"

"I have them, Assad!" yells Captain Galliotti, entering the room with Khalil and Tecla at his feet and Inez in his arms. "But we must get out of the house! Now!"

"MOMMA!" both children scream. Hearing their voices seems to bring Frances back to the reality of the situation unfolding as she hugs both children. The crashing sound of a building not too far away collapsing makes everyone jump.

"Hurry, follow me!" screams Captain Galliotti, Inez still in his arms as he leads everyone out the door of the bedroom, down the hallway and to the top of the stairs. Standing at the top of the stairs and looking down at the floor below is like witnessing a hallucination; the very stairs themselves seemed to be moving. A huge chandelier lay in pieces at the foot of the stairs. Without another moment's delay, Captain Galliotti leads Assad and his family down the stairs and out into the street. What Assad witnesses there is like witnessing Dante's Inferno. Entire blocks are reduced to nothing but mountains of rubble and the streets show fissures so wide several carriage, and horses have fallen into them. People are running everywhere, screaming out names while trying to avoid falling debris.

"You must get to the train station... quickly!" says Captain Galliotti as he hands Inez to Frances. Suddenly Inez screams, "I WANT DOLLY!" Evidently, she had left her doll in the bedroom during the confusion and she was terrified the doll would get hurt. Her mother tried to calm her down, "It's okay, Inez, Momma will get you another dolly."

"NO! I want Grand-poppa's dolly!" she wails, her body shaking. It was the doll the Captain gave her Christmas Eve and she had come to cherish it deeply.

"It's alright, little one, I'll go get it for you," the Captain says softly to Inez, his huge hand brushing back the hair from her face. And with that he rushes back into the crumbling building. "POPPA, NO!!" Frances wails.

From the time he entered the building until now seemed like hours to Assad as he looks up at the window of the bedroom, while also noticing a huge crack crawling up the side of the structure, threatening to bring it down at any moment. Once again the earth shifted beneath his feet and Assad is barely able to keep his balance.

"I HAVE IT!"

Assad looks up and sees Captain Galliotti leaning out the window, his hand clutching Inez's prized possession. "CATCH!" The dolly flutters in mid air then drops into Assad's hands like a gift from Heaven.

"Now hurry and get to the station," he bellows. "You have to get out of here as quick...." But he never finishes the command as the entire house seems to cave in on itself, the last vision Assad sees is the face of Captain Galliotti as tons of stone collapsed on him.

"POPPA!" shrieks Frances. "POPPA... NO!!"

Assad engulfs his entire family in his huge arms, Frances still crying as Inez holds her dolly tightly in her arms. "We have to get to the train station or we will all perish. Come!" Frances takes one last look at the house that now serves as a tomb. She blesses herself, looks up at Assad and slowly nods. "We have to save our children. So they can always remember their Grand-poppa," she said. Assad nods and kisses her on the forehead. "Yes, let's go."

CHAPTER SEVEN

April 1909

Testaccio, Italy

It is late morning as Assad sits quietly at the kitchen table, looking down at the newspaper spread out before him. The date on the top of the paper reads January 10, 1909, but some force within has compelled him to hold on to it all this time. Occasionally he would take it out of the bottom drawer of the dresser in his bedroom and read the story. Although the horrific events happened nearly four months ago, it felt as if he were reliving it each day, the images unable to be washed away with the passing of time. So once again, Assad looks down at the front page of the *Corriere della Sera* and reads unparalleled accounts of human tragedy:

Thousands Perish as Earthquake Levels Messina

MESSINA, ITALY (January 10, 1909)-- On Monday 28 December 1908, just before 5:30am, an earthquake of unprecedented fury laid waste to the busy port city of Messina.

At least 91% of structures in Messina were destroyed or irreparably damaged and some 75,000 people were killed in the city and suburbs.

It was the most destructive earthquake ever to strike Europe. The ground shook for up to 30 seconds, and the damage was widespread.

A young doctor who escaped with his life later recounted that "the profound silence was broken by an extraordinary noise like the bursting of a thousand bombs, followed by a rushing and torrential rain." Then he heard a "sinister whistling sound" which he likened to "a thousand red hot irons hissing in the water." Other survivors reported that there were three separate and different movements during the 30–40 second main shock: the first shaking backwards and forwards, the second thrusting violently upwards, with the third moving in a circular motion. All accounts concur that it was the second upwards motion that caused the widespread destruction in Messina; the accompanying noise described as having been "exactly like that made by a fast train in a tunnel".

The elevated death toll was due to the fact that most people were asleep, and killed outright or buried alive in their beds, as their houses collapsed on top of them. Thousands were trapped under debris, suffering horrific injuries of which many would die. Messina was even more crowded than usual, due to the number of overnight visitors from outlying areas who had come to the city to see a performance of Giuseppe Verdi's opera Aida, which had been staged the previous evening at the Vittorio Emanuele II Theatre.

About ten minutes after the earthquake, the sea on both sides of the Strait suddenly withdrew as a 40-foot tsunami swept in, and three waves struck nearby coasts. In Messina, the tsunami also caused more devastation and deaths; many of the survivors of the earthquake had fled to the relative safety of the seafront to escape their collapsing houses. The second and third tsunami waves, coming in rapid succession and higher than the first, raced over the harbor, smashed boats docked at the pier, and broke parts of the sea wall. After engulfing the port and three city blocks inland beyond the harbor, the waves swept away people, a number of ships that had been anchored in the harbor, fishing boats and ferries.

Afterwards Messina harbor was filled with floating wreckage and the corpses of drowned people and animals. About 2,000 people were killed by the tsunami in Messina.

Victims' bodies lying outside badly damaged and destroyed buildings in the port of Messina

A boys' boarding school was pulverized, burying the students. A total of 348 railway workers were killed when the two railway stations crumbled.

But in the throes of tragedy arose reports of heroism. A shopkeeper named Sergio Luciano, who led dozens of people to his store basement to save them as the buildings collapsed around them. He and the others were safely dug out after two days, safe and unharmed. Finally, all of Messina mourns the loss of Captain Giovanni Galliotti, one of Messina's leading citizens and philanthropists. It was reported that Captain Galliotti perished while undertaking the heroic and unselfish act of returning to his damaged home to retrieve a prized possession for his granddaughter. Sadly, he was not able to escape. All of Messina offers their prayers for the Captain and his family.

Assad takes off his glasses and rubs the spot between his eyes at the top of his nose, his body tense and rigid. He then does what he always does after reading the newspaper… he prays. It is only Frances' hands, gently kneading his corded shoulder muscles, that makes him relax.

"Assad, I don't know why you have to keep remembering that awful event?" He smiles at the sound of her voice. "I don't know, my love… but more important; how are you feeling today?"

For the past week or so, Frances had felt ill, to the point that she was unable to perform her teaching duties, which made her feel even worse. A neighbor had taken Khalil and Tecla to school this morning. Inez, Assad assumed, was still asleep.

"A little better," she replies, moving to the other side of the table and sitting down across from him. Assad looks at his wife; a mask of concern on his face. "Perhaps we should still contact Dr. Santini... just to make sure?"

Frances just smiles and reaches across the table. She takes his hands in hers and rests them on the newspaper. She looks down once at the headline, sighs softly, and then her eyes rise to meet Assad's as a small smile creeps across her face. She blushes slightly.

"I don't think we need Dr. Santini to tell me what I already know, husband." The blush darkened. "I am with child."

Assad realizes his jaw was slightly ajar. He took a breath, "A child? My God, that is *wonderful* news!"

"I know. I am thinking likely in December."

"A December baby," he says softly to himself. "December... what shall we name him... or her?"

"Well," said Frances slowly, "I was thinking if it is a boy that we would name him after my Poppa—Giovanni."

"And if it's a girl?"

"I like Lydia," she says, then adds quickly "Do you like Lydia? It's such a pretty name. Lydia. But if you don't like it, we can...."

"I love it," he says, smiling as he squeezes her hands ever so gently. "It's a beautiful name. Lydia"

Assad stands and crosses over to the stove, where he turns the flame up under an old tea kettle. "Now I have some news to share—though nothing as exciting as yours, of course," he adds with a chuckle.

"What is it?"

Assad adjusts the kettle slightly on the stove while collecting his thoughts. "I have been giving a lot of thought lately to our situation—our financial situation. We have been lucky so far that the good people of Testaccio have let us stay in this apartment rent-free, but we still have needs; food, clothing, the basic essentials. And although the church still pays me a small stipend since I left the priesthood, it's barely enough."

As the kettle starts to softly whistle, he removes it from the flame and continues. Frances watches him intently.

"I think it's time I acquired a skill, a trade, so to speak."

Frances spoke up, "But Assad, you have a skill. You comfort people, you give them hope, you help them see that they have a future in this world."

Assad smiles. "I know, and it's a skill I will hopefully always have. But I need something more... tangible, something that will help us be more comfortable, to provide for what we need—what our children need. Do you understand what I am saying, Frances?"

"I think so, that I understand," she answers, though Assad isn't one hundred percent sure she does. "But what would you do? What would be this skill that you would acquire?"

Assad thought a few minutes before he spoke, his memory now returning to a time many years ago, back to a small village in Lebanon. "You remember me telling you about my father, and how he used to sell furniture he carved out of the great cedar trees that surrounded my village?" Frances nodded.

"Well, occasionally he would take me on his deliveries. One day we made a stop in Beirut, at a small shop tucked away on a side street. It was store, a store that sold jewelry; men's watches, tie clips, ladies' bracelets, diamond necklaces. The owner, a wonderful man—I remember he gave me a string of licorice—needed a new desk for his back office. While my father was in the office I got to walk around the shop and marvel at the beautiful gems, mesmerized at how the light bounced off them. The effect was almost... *blinding*. I had never seen anything like it before. It was beautiful."

Assad paused and looked at his wife, who by now was smiling. "So, Assad, you want to own a ... jewelry store?"

"No, no... of course not. Where would I find the funds for such an endeavor, my beloved? What I am saying, and perhaps not very well, is that an opportunity has arisen that I may be able to work *in* a jewelry store, to learn the business."

"Opportunity?"

"Yes, a few days ago, in the marketplace while shopping for some supplies for the food kitchen, I just by chance started up a conversation with a nice elderly gentleman who was also there buying some vegetables. Come to learn, through our brief but enlightening talk, that his name was Chaim Stern, and many years ago he and his wife traveled here from their home in Jerusalem."

"And how does this chance meeting while buying squash and zucchini connect to working in a jewelry store?"

"Well, as fate would have it, Mr. Stern owns a jewelry store, in the Campo DiForio section of Rome. It is just he and his wife as they have no children. So I told him about visiting a jeweler back in Lebanon and how much I was infatuated by the business, and he asked if I was interested in working in his store a few days a week."

"But this Mr. Stern knows you are a priest? And I am assuming he is a Jew?"

"Yes, yes," Assad answers, perhaps more briskly than he had intended. He felt his patience starting to slip a little and he didn't like how it felt. "Of course, I had my collar on, but that didn't matter… it doesn't matter. This is something I would like to do, that I want to do. Not only for me but the extra money will help us."

Frances smiles and reaches across the table, the back of her hand caressing her husband's cheek. "Then that is what you should do. And although you are the priest in the family, I give you my blessing."

"What do you know about diamonds, Assad?"

Standing behind the counter in his store, Chaim Stern holds a small diamond in front of him between his fingers. He stares at the gem intensely. In the five months Assad has worked in Chaim's store he never fails to be both amused and intrigued at the love affair between the man and the precious stones he surrounded himself with. If his wife, Miriam, a wonderful woman, wasn't sure of the love her husband possessed for her, she would certainly be jealous. But they were both wonderful people, and Assad's children took to them immediately, almost as if adopting them as the grandparents they no longer had.

"The quality of a diamond is fashioned from the original crystal shape," Chaim continued. "It possesses a combination of brightness, sparkle, fire, and sense of purity not matched by other gems. A diamond is the only gem made of a single element: It is typically about 99.95% carbon. The other 0.05% can include one or more trace elements, which are atoms that aren't part of the diamond's essential chemistry. Some trace elements can influence its color or crystal shape." Assad wasn't crystal clear on exactly what the old jeweler was saying, but he listened intently.

"Whether fashioned or rough, and no matter what their shape, all diamonds have the same chemical composition and internal crystal structure." He turns his attention away from the gem and looks at Assad. "Did you know, Assad, that the way a mineral forms help determine its identity? Diamonds form under high temperature and pressure conditions that exist only within a specific depth range, perhaps 100 miles beneath the earth's surface. A diamond's crystal structure is isometric, which means the carbon atoms are bonded in essentially the same way in all directions. Another mineral, graphite, also contains only carbon, but its formation process and crystal structure are very different. The result is that graphite is so soft that you can write with it. But a diamond, Assad, a diamond is so hard…do you know the only thing that can scratch a diamond, Assad?" Assad simply shook his head. Chaim smiled…"Another diamond."

The jeweler put the diamond in a velvet box, where it would lay with various other gems. He hands it to Assad. "It is almost closing time, please put these back in the safe and we'll lock up." Assad nods and takes the box. He walks through the curtains and into the office where the safe is. But before he can complete his task he hears the door of the shop open, followed by loud voices.

"Hello, Jew. I believe you have some money for us."

Assad peeks through the curtains and sees two men standing in front of the counter. They are young, maybe in their late-twenties. One is big and broad shouldered and seems to be taking the lead. His partner is smaller and his eyes dart about as if someone might walk in at any moment. It is apparent to Assad that this is a shakedown of sorts, an attempt to extort money. His mine flashes back to that fateful day in his small kitchen and the menacing presence of Salim Al-Mahoud. And like that petty criminal, these two are bullies. And although as a priest Assad was taught never to hate his fellow man, bullies often tested his resolve. He knows what he has to do. He removes his collar and places it gently on the desk… best to confront the situation as a civilian, he thinks to himself. Assad takes a deep breath, parts the curtains and walks briskly back into the shop.

"Buona sera, gentlemen! How can I be of service?"

At the sudden appearance of Assad the two men are physically startled. It is a situation that is amplified by the fact that Assad stands just a hair over six feet two inches and his body is still heavily muscled, even in his late-30s.

"Who the hell are you?" the big man snarls.

"Just someone here to help you find what you need," Assad answers, sticking out his hand in a gesture of friendliness. The man, now sporting a confused look on his face, instantly offers his own hand, which is a mistake. Taking the man's hand in his, Assad slowly exerts serious pressure on the grasp. The man lets out a small grunt and his knees start to buckle slightly. "Perhaps I could help you find what you are looking for... perhaps for a girlfriend, or a wife?" With his right hand tightly holding on to the man, Assad's left arm loops around and he grips the man's neck. He walks him over to one of the cases. The man has no choice but to follow. "Perhaps a nice necklace or maybe a broche... how about a broche?"

The man shakes his head, "No, nothing... please let go of my hand."

"Maybe your friend is looking for something special?" But the friend had hastily departed. "Hmmm, he seems to have left. Maybe you should leave, also? What do you think?" The man, his face now red as a beet, hastily nods. Assad walks the man over to the door and pushes him through. The man stumbles, but regains his balance. He runs down the street without looking back. "Don't forget," Assad yells after him. "Tomorrow we are having a sale on gold men's collar clasps!"

Assad shuts the door behind him and turns to see Chaim standing behind the counter, smiling and shaking his head. "That was not very priestly, Assad," he says, still smiling.

"Oh, I don't know," Assad answers, trying to suppress his own smile. "He seemed like a very satisfied customer." Both men laugh.

Returning home that evening, Assad makes the decision not to tell Frances what had transpired at the store, in an effort not to get her too excited as she awaited the appearance of their next child. Their apartment was on the third floor of the building and the unrelenting late summer sun that had baked Testaccio all day had now stored within the stairwells like an oven. Assad could feel the sweat dripping down his back as he entered his apartment, only to be startled by the sight of portly Father Pietro sitting at his kitchen table drinking a glass of iced tea while dabbing his profusely sweating forehead with a wrinkled handkerchief. Frances is standing off to the side, her hands nervously wringing a dish towel. She smiles meekly at Assad.

"My God," the priest exclaims, "How can you bear this insufferable heat?"

"Father Pietro, so nice to see you, as always," says Assad. "But if I may ask, why are you here?"

Father Pietro put down his glass, stuffed the sweat-stained handkerchief back into his pocket, leans back in his chair and proceeds to fold his hands together over his ample stomach. He closed his eyes for a few minutes, and Assad wonders if perhaps the priest had fallen asleep, or maybe passed out from the heat. But then he quickly opens his eyes.

"I am here as a messenger, Assad, with a message for you."

"A message for me… from whom?"

Father Pietro lets a wide grin sweep across his face, as if for some time he had been imagining Assad asking that very question.

"Why, from The Holy Father, of course."

Assad jumps as Frances drops the cup she had been drying. The pieces lie at her feet, but she never even bothers to look down at them. "A message for Assad… from Pope Pius," she said slowly and subconsciously blesses herself.

"Yes, my dear Frances. It appears the Holy Father wishes to have Assad meet with him at the Vatican. Next week."

Assad is dumbstruck. He isn't even sure he is breathing, yet he has to ask, "Why does he want to meet with me?"

"Come now, Assad, who am I to question the motives of The Holy Father? I am sure it will all be clear once you meet with him." Father Pietro then adds, "And Frances, he wishes you to accompany Assad." Frances' jaw drops as the dish towel falls from her hand, landing next to the broken tea cup.

"Me? Meet The Pope? I can't... I shouldn't," she stammers.

"But why on earth not?" asks Father Pietro.

Frances blushes as she inches closer to Father Pietro, her voice dropping. "Because... I am with child."

Father Pietro looks at her for just a moment then burst out laughing, his jowls shaking. "My dear, I am sure His Holiness is well aware of the gifts God bestows on his children. You will be just fine." With that Father Pietro takes the napkin that was placed on the table in front of him and stuffs it in a very small space between his ample neck and collar.

"Now, is that a pecan pie I see sitting over there?"

A week later, a very nervous Assad and Frances sit on a bench outside the massive doors that serve as the office of Pope Pius X. They hold each other's hands. Neither speak, fully engrossed in the religious opulence that surrounds them, although for a brief moment Assad's mind flashes back to the glowing face of a young Frances on the boat when he first landed in Italy many years ago, and her exuberance that he might one day meet The Pope. Now here she was, meeting The Pope herself. The thought made him smile, but only for a moment as the massive doors opened and a priest bowed and invited them into the hallowed chambers.

As Assad and Frances enters they are awestruck by the room, which features a high ceiling ordained with gold figures and lush red velvet curtains on the wall. In the middle of the room is a large desk and rising from behind the desk to greet them is The Holy Father. He is a rather large man with white hair and an engaging smile. He wears the traditional garb of a red cloak over a white smock, a gold cross hangs demurely around his neck. He extends his right hand as both Assad and Frances kneel to kiss the ring. He smiles and asks them to join him on a huge couch with a table in front of it. Which they do. Now seated, The Pope speaks for the first time.

"I am sure you are wondering why I asked you here today," he says, his voice surprisingly soft for a large man. "First, Assad, I am aware that you have left the priesthood…"

"Holy Father, I can explain why…" Assad quickly injects. But The Holy Father merely smiles and holds up his hand. "It is fine; I know you have your reasons, and very good reasons. But let me continue, if I may." All Assad could do was nod in embarrassment.

"It has also come to my attention that for the past 10 years or so you have been doing exceptional work, God's work, in Testaccio. Why, I can remember when I first came to Italy from Austria I was appalled at the living conditions there; it was heart wrenching to think of people—men, women, children—living there in such squalid conditions." Pope Pius pauses and looks down at his hands. "And it hurts to think that perhaps the Catholic Church could have done more to help those poor people at that time. But we didn't." He then looks up into Assad's eyes. "But *you* did, Assad. For over 10 years you sacrificed your own comfort to help the people of Testaccio. You lived among them, felt their pain, their misery, and then you channeled those feelings back to them. Through your relentless hard work, and also that of Frances, you helped build schools, a clinic, a nursery for the children; your efforts in revitalizing Testacchio brought money back into the neighborhood to finish building the structures that would house these people, to give them once again hope and a sense of pride of community. To give them a neighborhood they are now proud to live in. And by doing so, by your sacrifice, you renewed their faith that God had not abandoned them. *You* did that, Assad."

Assad looks down at his hands folded now in his lap. "Holy Father... I... I don't know what to say."

"No need to say anything, my son. But allow me to reward you as only the Mother Church can." And with that he lifts his arm and instantly a priest is standing in front of the sofa, placing a small box on the table in front of Pope Pius, Assad and Frances.

It is a wooden box, maybe six inches by 10 inches, with a wooden slide top that opens the box. As The Pope opens the box, it reveals a small gold frame, and inside the frame is a glass case.

"This is a Holy Relic," says The Pope. "And something you must always treasure." He looks at the object and waives his hand slowly over it. "In the center of this case there is a chip of the cross that Our Savior was crucified on, surrounded by a chip of the bones of 29 saints.

 Accompanying it is all the appropriate documents speaking to its authenticity." He holds up the document to read it. "This is dated 1873, and was

re-authenticated in 1895." He puts the case and the document back in the box, closes it and hands it to Assad. Assad's hands tremble as he holds the case. He can hear Frances softly crying.

"Holy Father... I don't know what to say. Surely there are others far worthier to have bestowed on them such a sacred gift."

Pope Pius smiles. "Perhaps there are, Assad. But this I wanted you to have. But remember, you must guard it always. It is a treasure and you must treat it as such. You cannot sell it, you cannot give it away. If you choose to do so, it must be returned immediately to the Vatican. Do you understand?"

"I do, Holy Father."

The Pope rises, signaling that the meeting is over. Frances and Assad stand as well. "Now I have work I must attend to, as I must now meet with people that are not nearly as interesting as you are," he says with a smile. He then turns to Frances, who Assad thought was going to faint at any second.

"And I see you are with child, how wonderful." And with that he proceeds to bestow a blessing on her for a safe and healthy delivery. The tears roll down her cheek but she still manages to smile and eke out a soft, "Thank you, Holy Father. We shall never forget this day."

On a warm spring night in April of 1910, Assad and Frances had just finished a lovely dinner, having hosted Chaim and Miriam at their home. Frances is washing the last of the dishes while Khalil, Tecla and Inez play in their room. The newest addition to the family, Lydia Concetta Elizabeth Hajjar, who had entered the world just four months prior on December 4, 1909, sleeps peacefully on Miriam's ample bosom as she sits in a large overstuffed chair. Chaim and Assad sit across from each other at the table, sipping wine and looking down at the latest newspaper. Chaim is emotionally in full throttle as talk turns to what is beginning to unfold; *war*.

"I am telling you Assad," Chaim bellows, jamming his finger into the newspaper, there are some bad things starting to happen, and you can tie it right back to Luigi Luzzatti replacing

Sidney Sonnino last month as Prime Minister, and the dammed socialists that are starting to pop up everywhere!"

"Chaim, please, your blood pressure," urges Miriam. But Chaim just waves his hand dismissively.

"Never mind my blood pressure, woman… there are more important things to talk about.

"Calm down, my friend," offers Assad. "You may be just working yourself up over some small talk."

"Small talk," says Chaim. "*Small talk…* have you not been reading the papers, man! I am telling you war is coming!" He takes a breath and a large gulp of wine. Then he continues.

"This madman, Lozzatti, is riling people up by telling them as the heir of the Roman Empire, Italy is entitled to rule over former Roman territories. And since Libya was the sole Mediterranean region not claimed by another European power, it should belong to Italy."

"But that doesn't mean the people, or the cabinet will agree," says Assad.

But Chaim would not let up. "Don't you see, Luzzatti is viewing Libya as Italy's "Fourth Shore", and that by invading Libya it will solve Italy's high unemployment and emigration issue by settling poor Italians there. He is telling the people what they want to hear. And I am hearing that by next spring we could be landing up to a million troops in North Africa"

"A million troops," says Frances, who was obviously now caught up in the conversation. "But how does that affect us, affect Assad?"

Chaim tries to contain his impatience. "Don't you see child, those troops need to come from somewhere, which means... do you know what *conscription* is?" Frances shook her head no. "Conscription is when the government orders you to fight in the military. And, trust me, they will have their eyes on the lookout for strong able bodies to do the fighting, whether those individuals want to or not."

Frances was starting to understand the direction the conversation was going in and it began to frighten her. "You mean, they could make Assad go fight in the war?"

With that Assad rose and went over to Frances, holding her in his arms. "Now we can't think like that," he says softly. "Why would they want a 35-year old priest going into battle with a Bible?" But it was Chaim who answered.

"What they *want*, Assad, is a 35-year old with the body of a 25-year old going into battle with a rifle."

Suddenly it was all beginning to dawn on Assad that by next year he could be away from his family fighting in a war, a war being fought not far from the very land he left many years ago. "So you are saying we should... leave? Leave Italy?"

"That's exactly what I am saying, my friend."

"But go... where?"

Chaim reaches into his inside pocket and produces an envelope, which he then places on the newspaper on the table. Assad walks over and looks down at it, but does not reach for it. "What's that?"

"That, Assad, is all the information you will need to take your family away from what is sure to be a terrible coming of events. My brother owns a jewelry store and I have already spoken to him about working with you when you get there. But you must be ready because it is a long journey across a vast expanse of water."

Assad shakes his hand, "Chaim, I appreciate it, but I have no desire to travel *back* across the Mediterranean to Jerusalem." And with that, all Chaim could do was chuckle.

"No, Assad. The Mediterranean is but a mere drop in the bucket. I am talking about the Atlantic Ocean. I came to Italy, but my brother, Emil, he and his family migrated to South America, to Argentina."

"Argentina," Assad repeats. "Live in Argentina?"

"Don't look so surprised," Chaim offers. "A good friend of ours works on the docks in Genoa and he tells us thousands of Italians have chosen Argentina as their new adopted land, even more than those choosing to go to America." Chaim smiles. "You'll feel right at home." But then he took on a serious tone.

"Assad, you must go, and soon. I took the liberty of making all the arrangements with the ship line. The ship departs the first of next month."

Assad didn't know what to say. "Ship... but how will we pay for it. We don't have enough..." Chaim stopped him there.

"It's all paid for; I took care of it." And before Assad could object, as Chaim knew his friend would, he said, "Listen, Assad, Miriam and I came to this country with no one. We never had any children. But in the brief time we have known you, and Frances and the children; you have made us all feel like family. And family, for my people, means everything. This is our gift to you." Assad looks deeply into the eyes of his friend and he can see the forming of tears.

"And," Chaim continues, "our gift is knowing you are all safe and well." He hands Assad the envelope. "Promise me you will go." Assad looks over at Frances. She nods. He then turns back to Chaim, bends down and kisses the elderly man on his forehead.

"We will go, Chaim. But know that you and Miriam will always be with us. *Wherever we are.*"

Chaim looks up to his friend, picks up his glass of wine, and says softly, *"L'Chaim."*

When he sees the quizzical look on Assad's face, he explains. "It means… 'To life'."

CHAPTER EIGHT

September 1910

Buena Aires, Argentina

It takes Assad and his family a mere five days to cross the Atlantic. Thanks to Chaim's generosity they are able to book passage on the steamship *Tomasso di Faucia*, with fairly comfortable accommodations, departing from the Port of Genoa. Assad is quick to acknowledge that it was a far more pleasant voyage than the one that took him from Lebanon to Italy a dozen years ago. And they hardly felt like strangers; most of the ship's passengers were also Italians looking for a new life in Argentina, which was seeing a tremendous influx of immigration from Europe. There were reports of already tens of thousands of Italians who had made the journey across the ocean, although Assad felt that perhaps that number was getting inflated with each passing mention.

Once the boat docked in the busy Buenos Aires port, Assad, his family safely in tow—Frances, Khalil, Tecla, Inez and baby Lydia—he is quickly rescued from the teeming masses that are engulfing him by a most jovial Emil Stern, just as his old friend, Chaim, had promised. Emil grabbed some of Assad's belongings under his arm and directed them to a carriage which quickly navigated the crowd with surprising ease. Soon they were away from the noise and smells of the docks and doing a leisurely pace on the cobblestone streets of La Bocca, a small but friendly neighborhood just outside Buenos Aires where many of the immigrants from Italy had come to call home. Emil had arranged for Assad and his family to stay with them. His home was big and could accommodate a family the size of Emil's. Sadly, it was only Emil and his 14-year old daughter, Rebecca—who he called Beca—as his wife had not survived the journey from Israel to South America. Assad resisted this hospitality at first, but he quickly relented when he could see in Emil's eyes that he would welcome the company. And it took no time for Beca—whom Frances suspected had a crush on Assad—to warm up to Assad's family, and she adored the children, who immediately took to her as well.

As smoothly as Assad adapted to his new surroundings, and enjoyed his time working with Emil in his jewelry store in Buenos Aires, Frances was not as quick to adapt. She often seemed lost, tucked away in her own thoughts. Assad knew how much she missed her father, and in some ways the death of her first born still weighed heavily on her, still, Assad felt this morose was tied into something else much deeper.

One day in the fall of 1911, Assad had come home for lunch and the first thing he heard was Lydia crying in one of the bedrooms, her wailing so strong she was gasping for air. "Frances," he cried out, but no response came. He hurried into the bedroom only to find Lydia lying on her back crying, her diaper soiled with feces covering the top part of her legs. Assad hurried over to pick up the child, whose cries diminished with the familiar touch of her father's hands. He quickly cleaned the child off with a damp rag and changed her into a clean diaper. "But where was Frances," he thought, now starting to worry. Had she gone out and left her baby alone? She would never.

Assad carried Lydia into one of the other bedrooms, where he found Frances sitting in a chair, staring out the window. She appeared deep in thought, so intense that at one point Assad wasn't sure she was even breathing.

"Frances?" he said softly. She did not acknowledge him. He took a few steps closer.

"My love, is everything okay? Lydia… she was crying. Did you not hear her?"

Frances turned and looked at her husband. She smiled and held out her hands for Lydia. For one moment Assad hesitated handing her the child, but then passed her to Frances. She looked down at the child, who by now had literally cried herself to sleep. "My beautiful child. Isn't she beautiful, Assad?"

Assad smiled. "Yes, Frances, she is beautiful." He put his hand on his wife's shoulder. "And you, Frances, are *you* okay?" Frances looked up, her face now masked in bewilderment. "Of course I am husband. Why wouldn't I be?" She looked down again at Lydia, who was now purring soundly. "Would you please make me a cup of tea?"

Assad studied his wife's face. It was as if nothing had happened. But he was still troubled.

"Of course, my love," Assad replied. And with that he turned and exited the bedroom, still deep in thought.

"I'm telling you, Emil, it was if she was a thousand miles away. And I have to admit, it frightened me a little."

Assad recounted the events of the day to Emil when he returned to the jewelry store that Chaim's brother owned and operated on a side street in downtown Buenos Aires. Assad had begun working at the shop right after arriving in Argentina, and just as he had while working with Chaim, he enjoyed it immensely. Emil put down the instrument he was using to polish some of the gems and looked up at his new friend.

"You must understand Assad that Frances has endured quite a lot in a relatively short period of time. She has lost her father, lost a child, and had to pack up her entire life and travel to a new country." Emil stood up and returned the gems to their glass case. "And from what I understand from Chaim's letters, Frances was very active in her old neighborhood—I believe she even taught at the school, is that correct?"

"Yes, that's true."

"Now here she is; Tecla, Inez and Khalil are in school, and she is home all day alone with Lydia. Maybe she feels like she has more to offer."

Assad let out a sigh and leaned on the glass case with both hands. "Perhaps you are right… but what are the alternatives?"

"You may not have noticed it, seeing as you have only been in Buenos Aires for a short time, but there is a wave of support growing on behalf of women," offered Emil. "To make their voices stronger on behalf of social change, perhaps even securing the right to vote."

"And how would this help Frances and her situation?" Assad asked. "I don't understand."

Emil smiled patiently. "A very good customer of mine was a woman—a very strong-willed woman—by the name of Virginia Bolton. And about 10 years ago, maybe a little more, she started a paper called *La Voz de la Mujer*, which was the first feminist paper in all of Argentina. And this newspaper would raise issues such as domestic violence, divorce and, of course, the right for women to vote." He continued, "Needless to say, there were those who felt her views tipped the scales more towards anarchy and socialism, and she developed some enemies." And with a chuckle he added, "Of course, when your motto is 'No God, No Master, No Husband,' people start to take notice. But she did manage to attract a lot of attention and a lot of followers."

"I don't know Emil," Assad said with some hesitancy, "it all sounds a little… dangerous."

109

"My dear, Assad, I am not advocating that our Frances run around throwing bombs, just that maybe it would give her a sense of pride to be involved with a rising tide of change that seems to be coming, that perhaps it will instill in her a new sense of pride. And I am sure Beca would be happy to watch Lydia for a few hours a day."

Assad had to admit listening to Emil that he was warming to the idea of Frances once again being involved in doing something for others, a trait that made her beloved in Testaccio. "And you want Frances to meet with this Bolton woman?"

Emil let out a hearty chuckle as he walked over to the door of the shop, turned the latch and flipped the CLOSED sign. "Not unless you plan on traveling to Uruguay." Noting the look of confusion on Assad's face, he continued. "She was deported in 1902. But there are many who have continued her teachings, particularly this woman." Emil scribbled on a piece of paper and handed it to Assad. The note contained a name and address.

"Elvira Rawson de Dellepiane," Assad read.

"Yes," Emil responded. "A most remarkable woman. About four years ago she founded the Feminist Center. And I know for a fact she is always looking for help from strong-minded women… which I know Frances most assuredly is."

Assad folded the note and put it in his breast pocket. He thanked his friend, grabbed his coat and headed to the back door of the shop; still not 100% convinced this was the right course of action. But then he thought to himself, "Maybe she will embrace the opportunity. We shall see."

By winter of 1912, it had become apparent to Assad that Frances not only embraced this opportunity to lend her voice to a strong cause, she gulped it down like water given to a thirsty man in the desert. It was not uncommon for Assad to come home at night to a dinner table void of food but festooned with markers and posters expounding messages about a "woman's right to vote" and "down with domestic violence." Even at nine-years old, Tecla was already helping her mother by organizing pamphlets and flyers on the kitchen floor, Assad couldn't help but notice the passion in his wife's voice and the admiration in her eyes as she spoke of Elvira Rawson de Dellepiane.

"Assad, you will not meet a more remarkable woman," she explained excitedly. "She was only the second woman in all of Argentina to become a doctor, and with her degree became an activist for women's and children's rights. She even worked in the hospital helping the wounded soldiers during the Revolution of 1890." Assad just smiled, but let Frances continue to have her jubilant moment. "And after all that, she now holds the title of Medical Inspector for the Department of National Health."

Frances paused a moment to collect her thoughts, but there was no stopping her. "The women I have met... I can't tell you how impressed I am with their commitment to righting the wrongs that women have been subjected to over the years. And it's not just stifling our right to vote, it's also how men have turned their head when the subject of abuse comes up, whenever the issue turns to protecting wives who are being beaten by their husbands, or worse. It's terrible."

Assad could see Frances was starting to get worked up, her face turning a light shade of crimson. "Frances, dear, calm down. I am happy you have found an outlet for your passion, but I am still a little worried. After all, there are elements out there who feel the movement is, let's say... a bit too anarchistic."

Her eyes spit fire, Assad took a step back as Frances unleashed her tirade.

"What people are you talking about, Assad? Are these the same people who slap their wives if the dinner is late coming to the table? Are these the same cowards who punch their wives if they find a hole in their sock? Are they, Assad...? TELL ME!"

Assad tried to calm his wife down, her breathing now slow and heavy. "Please, my love, calm yourself.... I only meant that..." But she interrupted him with a voice that was now *eerily* calm.

"I swear to you on my father's grave, Assad, if any man ever harmed my daughters, or treated them with disrespect, I would take a knife and plunge it into their black heart... and I would laugh while doing it." With that she turned and stormed into the bedroom, slamming the door behind her and leaving Assad speechless, and a little worried.

CHAPTER NINE

November 1912

Buenos Aires, Argentina

As far as Assad could tell, Frances had never seemed in better spirits. She was still high on the jubilation of helping Julieta Lanteri, a feminist activist, become the first Latin American woman to be allowed to vote last fall. It had been an historical milestone and Frances' woman's group was elated at the outcome. As a matter of fact it had been the impetus to accelerate their efforts to give women more voice and more power. But not everyone shared their enthusiasm.

Standing in Emil's jewelry store watching a heavily-bosomed middle-aged woman holding up a diamond-studded necklace she was contemplating buying for her daughter's 21st birthday, Assad thought back to what unfolded earlier this year, and it made him shudder.

It was early evening on September 21 and Frances was on her way home from a meeting of her group. Not more than four blocks from her house she suddenly found herself surrounded by four men, who she would describe later to the police as "sweaty and smelly." They warned her that it was best for her health if she and her radical friends back off from all the "agitation," that some people didn't appreciate their point of view—"not that they would ever threaten her family."

Well, that just about lit the fuse. According to police reports she landed her heavy handbag across the face of one of her assailants, the metal claps opening up a gash in his cheek. But before she could follow up with another blow, she was clubbed to the ground.

"Excuse me... can you tell me how many karats these stones are? They are for my daughter, you know?"

The customer's booming voice brought Assad back to the present. "I'm sorry...?"

"These diamonds," repeated the woman, her voice tinged in impatience. "Are they good quality? I want only the best for my Eva."

"Madam, I assure you... these stones are of the finest cuts. And I am sure they will look wonderful on your daughter, especially if she is as beautiful as you."

The woman blushed and giggled like a teenager at the compliment from the handsome Assad. "I believe I will take them. Please have them sent to my home." She paused. "Or feel free to deliver them yourself."

"Of course, madam," Assad answered, bowing graciously. After the woman left Assad continued to recall how he received a call from the police the previous night telling him that Frances was at the station and she had been assaulted. But she was fine as several men came along and chased her attackers off before any real damage could be done. They then drove her to the local station. Assad found her there, slightly bruised but in better spirits than he had expected. He was amazed to see her sitting at the police sergeant's desk sharing a cup of tea with the officer, as if nothing happened.

A hot, dusty summer of 1913 flew by as Assad marveled at watching Frances continue her commitments to her group and the children growing in what seemed like leaps and bounds. 11-year old Tecla and eight-year old Inez were doing what sisters always do at that age, they were fighting over whose clothes were whose. Meanwhile Khalil, who at 13-years-old was already starting to grow beyond his years as it was becoming more and more evident that he would fill out like his father had, recently joined a local youth soccer program and seemed to be enjoying it. Assad had watched a few games and thought his son was a standout, even though he had yet to score a goal.

Lydia, all but three now, was still spending a lot of time with Emil's daughter, Beca, and they both seemed to be enjoying each other's company. Assad could not remember when life seemed so good. Still, it only got better when Frances announced to him that she was with child, a gift from God that would be entering the world early in the spring of 1914.

But alas, as Assad had come to learn since the day he was forced to flee his beloved Lebanon, He giveth and He taketh away.

On a chilly January morning, a few days after celebrating the ushering in of 1914, Assad was awakened from a deep sleep by heavy knocking at the front door. Still trying to shake the slumber from his head, he sat up in bed and listened, wanting to make sure the sound was real and not just an echo from a dream. But there was no mistaking it was real when he heard more pounding and a frantic voice he recognized as belonging to Beca.

"ASSAD! ASSAD! OPEN UP!"

Pulling on his pants and pulling his suspenders up over his shoulders, he then slipped his feet into his slippers.

"Assad, is that Beca?" he heard his wife murmur as she lay beside him, her very pregnant stomach on its side facing away from him.

"Yes, my beloved. Go back to sleep."

Assad went through the kitchen and unlatched the wooden door. As he opened it Beca literally threw herself into his arms. "Beca... what's wrong? What's going on?"

"It's my father," she managed to get out through the sobbing.

"Emil? What's wrong with Emil? Tell me what's going on."

"We have to get to the hospital, Assad. Please..." she cried, pulling at his arm. "I will tell you everything on the way. Hurry!"

Not more than 30 minutes later Assad and Beca entered the prestigious *Hospital de Clinicas*, a teaching institution associated with the University of Buenos Aires. It was in Room 472 that Assad found his friend, Emil. He was hooked up to an oxygen machine and there was a monitor strapped to his chest. His face was ashen and haggard and his chest heaved slightly. Assad's heart sank.

On the way to the hospital Beca explained that she and her father had gone to the shop to open up this morning and as soon as Emil unlocked the door a man, who had apparently been waiting outside, pushed the door open, brandishing a shotgun with the intent of robbing the store. Beca explained that she was terrified but her father refused to open the store safe even after the man put the shotgun to his head. But before anything else could happen, Emil suddenly fell over clutching his chest, apparently in the full throes of a massive heart attack. As Beca screamed out to her father who now was lying on his back and struggling to breathe, the robber, at this time scared out of his wits, broke a glass counter with the handle of the shotgun, grabbed some watches and bracelets, and ran out of the shop. Beca called the police who then sent an ambulance that transported Emil to the hospital while she ran to get Assad.

"Assad… is that you?"

Assad walked over to the bed and took his friend's hand. To Assad it seemed unusually cold. "I am here, my friend."

"Assad," said Emil, as he struggled to breathe. "My will is in the safe, at the shop. Beca has the combination."

"Hush, Emil… there is no need to talk about wills. You'll be back in the shop in no time." But Emil just shook his head and tightened his grip on Assad's hand as best he could. He could hear Beca softly sobbing.

"No, listen to me, Assad. Everything is spelled out in those papers; all my wishes." Emil closed his eyes, his breath coming in jagged spurts. A nurse entered the room. "I think it's best if we let him rest. You can come back tomorrow."

Assad looked down at his friend then put his arm around Beca. "We better go. But maybe we should stop at the shop first." Beca looked up into his face, her own streaked with tears, she sadly nodded her head. They left the room engulfed in their own individual sorrow.

Sadly, that was the last time Assad saw Emil alive as he suffered a second heart attack a few days after being admitted to the hospital and died in the middle of the night. Assad wrote Chaim in Rome to tell him the bad news. It was one of the hardest letters he had ever written.

The will that Assad and Beca picked up the day they left the hospital was all signed and legal, but nonetheless disturbing. In it, Emil passed ownership of the jewelry store to Assad, who almost immediately had a panic attack as he knew nothing about running a business. Emil had also left his house to Assad, with the stipulation that Beca would always have a place there. But Beca, who also received a good sum of money in the will, opted instead to move in with her aunt in Rio De Janeiro, knowing full well that Assad already had his hands full, especially with another child on the way.

Suddenly, at the age of 40, Assad Hajjar now found himself married, the father of four children (soon to be five), and a business owner. The thought terrified him.

"I was very sorry to hear about Emil. I had known him for years… a very sweet man."

The man offering his condolences was named Rudolph Klausman. Klausman was a German national who sold wholesale diamonds on the jewelry circuit stretching from South America up to North America. Emil was one of his best customers and they had worked together for over 15 years. "And you are the new owner, I assume?"

Assad extended his hand to Klausman, who was maybe 10 years older than Assad and at least a foot shorter. He wore a stylish suit and had a pair of glasses hanging around his neck on a chain. "I'm Assad Hajjar and, yes, I guess I am." The man's handshake was surprisingly strong. "It is a pleasure to meet you Assad. I look forward to working with you."

The gentleman put his briefcase on the counter but didn't open it. He looked at Assad deep in thought. "You say your last name is 'Hajjar'… is that a common name in Argentina?"

Assad couldn't resist a smile. "Not so much in Argentina. But if you are ever in Lebanon, we're all over the place there." Klausman returned the smile.

"I only ask because I do a lot of business in the jewelry district in New York City and one of the managers of a shop I do a lot of business with is also named Hajjar. Do you think there's any connection?"

Assad gave it some thought. "I mean, sure, it's possible. I know my father had many brothers and cousins throughout Lebanon and Syria, and many of them did migrate to America."

Klausman took a small notebook and pen out of his breast pocket. "Tell you what; let me jot down his name and address. Who knows; maybe someday you'll tire of the beautiful country and set out on a new adventure in a new country? It's certainly an amazing place." He tore off the slip of paper and handed it to Assad, who looked at it briefly and put it in his trouser pocket. "Thank you," he offered. "Perhaps that time will come. Now, why don't you show me what you have for me, Mr. Klausman." The German offered a wide smile and spread his arms. "Please, call me Rudy."

As winter slipped into spring, Assad felt like he was drowning in the sea of paper receipts on the table in front of him. He looked down at the table and put his hands to each side of his head, which he slowly shook. "I was never meant to own a

123

business," he moaned. "I have no idea what I am doing and because I don't know what I am doing I feel like we are losing money month to month."

A very pregnant Frances, due to give birth in a month or so, stood at the stove stirring a pot of sauce, one hand resting on her protruding stomach. The children were in their rooms either doing homework or playing with their toys.

"Perhaps you are being too hard on yourself," she offered.

"I don't know, maybe you are right."

"Assad."

"I mean, I like selling jewelry. But all this paperwork... it just doesn't come naturally."

"Assad."

"Maybe we should just sell the business…"

"ASSAD!"

"What…," he looked over at the horrified face of his wife. He then followed her eyes to the floor, where blood was running down her legs and pooling around her shoes.

"I think I should go to the hospital."

Like a shot Assad leaped from his chair as receipts went flying off the table in all directions. A bad day had just gotten worse.

Frances lay in her bed, a place she had been frequenting more and more since she lost her child just over a week ago. The doctor said she was fine now and would still be able to produce children. But Assad knew in his heart that it was hard for a mother to lose one baby, but two babies... it was time to make some important decisions.

Assad sat down on the side of the bed. How are you feeling, my love?" Frances shrugged. "Okay."

"I'd like to have a very important discussion with you, but I can only do it if I know, beyond a doubt, that you comprehend *exactly* what I am saying. Can you do that?"

Frances looked up at Assad, her mouth almost in a pout, "Of course I can. What do you think me, a child?" Assad smiled and took her hand. "Of course not. But we may have to make a big decision."

"What decision?"

Assad stood and began to pace the room. He rubbed the back of his neck with both hands, as if trying to wring the tension from his neck and shoulders.

"About a month or so ago a diamond wholesaler came into the shop; a wonderful gentleman. And we started talking and when he heard my name was Hajjar it reminded him that he had a customer in America—in New York City—with the same name."

"New York City?"

"Yes, yes," Assad continued. "He gave me this person's name and address and I wrote him a letter explaining who I was, where I was from, who my parents were; just to see if perhaps we were related in some way."

"And?"

"Well," said Assad, his voice now taking on a small level of excitement, "he wrote me back. I got his letter a few days ago." Assad took the letter from his trouser pocket and held it up. "It could be the key to a new future for us. With no worries, no cares, just peace of mind." He sat back down on the bed. "Think of it, Frances… *America!*"

Frances sat up higher on the bed and took the letter from Assad. She opened it, looked once more up at her husband, and read:

September 2, 1914

From: Mr. Nabih Hajjar
95 Monticello Avenue
Camden, New Jersey

Dear Assad,

How very nice to receive your letter, because for a brief moment it reminded me of home.

My father was a sheep herder in the southern part of Lebanon, and from what I know there is a good chance my father and your father were, at the very least, second cousins. Which means that in some way, yes, we are related.

I have also heard that we may have more relatives in the United States; in New York, New Jersey and even Massachusetts.

There are more and more immigrants coming through Ellis Island every day, and the population here continues to grow. Not only Lebanese and Syrians, but Italians, Germans, even the Irish. They come for freedom and opportunity. Yes, they must carve out these things for themselves, and it is hard work, but Assad, this is America. It is the land of opportunity.

It sounds like you have a wonderful family, and I would hope someday to meet them. Should you ever feel like your family would thrive in this new land, then I would be more than happy to help you find an apartment and honest employment. As a matter of fact, I am good friends with a foreman here in Camden who works at a factory—a soup factory—and I know they are always looking for strong, able-bodied workers.

Again, thank you for writing, my new-found cousin. And I look forward to your response.

Nabih

Frances folded the letter and put it on the nightstand.

"You want to move our family to America and make soup in… *she looked once more at the letter…* in New Jersey?" Assad nodded.

"I don't believe I would actually be *making* soup; probably help making the cans that the soup goes in, or maybe loading the trucks with the soup cans… I don't know." He gripped both her hands in his. "Don't you see, Frances. This is an opportunity for to make a fresh start, away from bad memories, with more chances for our children to be whatever they want to be."

"What about the jewelry store?" she asked.

"I already have a man, a Pakistani, who owns several shops outside Buenos Aires and he has been looking to open another shop here. He has offered me a fair price."

"And this house we live in?"

Assad slowly shook his head. "This house was a gift from Emil; I could never sell it. I will sign the deed over to Beca and she can do with it as she pleases."

Frances put one hand on the side of Assad's face. "This is what you want, husband?" He put his hand on hers. "This is what I want... but for us."

Frances smiled and laid her head back on the pillow. She turned on her side, away from Assad, and said in a soft voice. "Then this is what we will do."

Three weeks later Assad stood on the bustling docks that brought him to Argentina nearly four years ago. He was bundled up in his overcoat to the point of already sweating, but he knew when he got to America the late-October days would be a lot colder. His battered brown leather bag hung at his side. He looked up at the giant steamship.

Although the night before had almost turned ugly with arguments going back and forth, eventually it was agreed that the best course of action would be for Assad to travel by himself to the United States, for the purpose of establishing a residence and gaining employment. Reluctantly, Frances had agreed.

Assad said his goodbyes that night before the children went to bed—giving Inez, Tecla, and Lydia hugs and kisses. Khalil, who was already becoming a young man, chose to give his father a firm handshake. Early in the morning, when the children were still asleep, he made love to his wife for the first time in many months, then took the bag of sandwiches she had made the night before, and walked out the door to... America.

CHAPTER TEN

December 1914

Ellis Island, NY

The trip from Argentina had been long and arduous, but to Assad it seemed like every trip he's made since leaving Lebanon as a young man had gotten easier and easier. Still, the thought of Frances and the children doing the trip without him sent a shiver through him. But he knew it was best to be settled before they came. Of course the shiver could have been the result of an icy blast coming off the East River. Assad had his first taste of what winter truly means.

As he pulled his coat tighter around him he found himself being moved in a great line of passengers coming off the ship and being literally herded into a large stone building; there had to be thousands of people, all clutching children or suitcases, or both. Inside the hall was immense, with high ceilings and several balcony levels. There were dozens of long lines leading up to men sitting at tables. Assad was not sure which one to get into, so he chose the closest one.

"My guess is the first thing they will do is make sure we are healthy," came a voice from behind him. Assad turned slightly to his left and looked over his shoulder as a young man, perhaps in his early 20s, grinned at him. He wore a cap pulled down over his eyes and he chewed on the end of a plastic straw. "You sound like you've done this before," answered Assad. The man chuckled.

"Hardly. But my sister came over from Genoa a few months ago and she wrote me a letter pretty much describing what to expect."

"And what should I expect?"

"Well, she said the first thing would be a medical exam by military surgeons, but don't get nervous because they are dressed like soldiers, it's just their uniform."

Assad looked around and he could see the gentleman was correct in his assessment.

"You can see how this would confuse many people from other countries," the man continued. "Especially those from places where the military can be—shall we say—less than friendly."

Assad nodded. "And what happens when we get to the front of the line?"

"Well," the man continued. "First thing, they will check your papers against the manifest from the ship. If everything is *coppice*, then the doctors will examine you quickly for any type of eye disease, skin disorders, and heart disease, whatever they can find."

"And if they find something?"

"Then they draw a large letter on your clothes with a piece of chalk." The man used his finger to pantomime drawing a letter on Assad's shoulder. "The letter 'H' could mean you have a bad heart; 'L' they think you might be lame; or they could draw an 'X', and you don't want that."

"What does 'X' mean," Assad asked, not sure he wanted to know the answer.

"The letter 'X' means feeble-mindedness and those people get stuck here for sometimes up to a week, and then they could very well get sent right back home."

"But don't worry," Assad's new friend continued. "I am told that 90% get through this line of questioning without any problem. I guess because the doctors know there isn't enough space to detain too many people. What I find remarkable is that very few immigrants at Ellis Island, people like you and me, are ever denied entry to the United States. The irony here is that

133

you have this massive inspection process, and you know they are looking for criminals and anarchists and whatever, all these people you want to keep out of the country, and at the end of the day, less than 10% are rejected." The man laughed a loud laugh. "America! I love it!"

Having both passed their medical inspection, Assad shook hands and bid farewell to his new friend. Assad, now clutching his documents which said pretty much welcome to America, felt his arm being tugged. He looked to see a frantic old man, his eyes wide with fright, his long gray beard hanging almost down to his chest.

"ikh ken nisht gefinen meyn froy!," the man blurted out.

Assad, who was versed in many languages, could not comprehend what the man was saying, or in what language he was speaking. "I am sorry… I don't understand." But this response only made the man more agitated as he swiveled his head as if looking for someone. *"ikh ken nisht gefinen meyn froy!"*

Assad, determined to try and keep the man calm, said softly. "Come with me." He took the man gently by the arm and led him to a table where a very official gentleman was seated. "I will find someone to help you."

Assad and the man approached the gentleman at the table. He was a handsome young man, his hair neatly parted down the middle. He sat scribbling notes on a pad of paper.

"Excuse me, sir. Can you help us?" The man looked up. He smiled. "How may I assist you?"

Assad gestured to the old man, who was now on the brink of tears. "He is talking in a language I do not recognize." He gestured to the man to repeat what he had said to the man sitting at the desk. *"ikh ken nisht gefinen meyn froy!"*

The man at the desk nodded and replied, *"tsi nit zorg. mir veln gefinen ir."* The older gentleman visibly relaxed. *"zitsn dort aun ikh vel zeyn mit ir in etlekhe minut,"* added the younger man, who was obviously an interpreter. The elderly gentleman smiled and walked over to a chair, where he sat calmly. Assad was amazed.

"What did he say… and in what language was he saying it?" asked Assad.

"He was looking for his wife, who somehow got separated from him. And he was speaking Yiddish."

Assad smiled and shook his head. "And you just happen to speak Yiddish?" The man replied. "My father is Italian, but my mother is Jewish, from Austria-Hungary." The man held out his hand. "Forgive my rudeness, my name is Fiorello LaGuardia." Assad gripped the man's strong right hand. "Assad Hajjar. It's a pleasure to meet you. How long have you worked here?"

"I actually worked here full-time from about 1907 to 1910," Fiorello replied. "Then I left to study law at night school. I fill in every now and then when they need me... or if I need a little extra spending money." He looked over at the man in the chair, still waiting patiently. "Well, I guess I better get back to work. It was nice meeting you, Assad. And I wish you happiness with your new life in America." And with that he was off to fulfill his duties.

Standing outside Assad rested his hands on the brass railing and looked out at the river as a light snow started to fall. He could barely take his eyes of the image of the Statue of Liberty seemingly rising from the sea like the great Poseidon. He was mesmerized by how a simple statue could become a beacon of hope for hundreds of thousands of immigrants.

"Pretty impressive isn't it?"

Assad turned and saw a man about his age, with a thick black mustache and dark hair. He was about Assad's height but showing about 25 more pounds most of it around the middle. But he had a winning smile. Assad thought the description he was sent in one of the letters was dead-on.

"Cousin Nabih?" The smile on the man's face widened and that said it all. The two men embraced.

"How was your journey," Nabih asked, reaching down for Assad's bag. "Not too horrible, I hope? Come, there is a small boat that will take us across the river to New Jersey. Christ, it's freezing!" Assad could only smile as he never told his new-found family member that he was a priest. Nabih led the way, but not before Assad took one last look at the Great Lady and all she promised for his family.

It was a very short ride across the river and Assad was amazed to see what was waiting for them. He had always assumed

Nabih would have a horse and wagon, so he was surprised when he saw an automobile. Nabih laughed when he saw the look on Assad's face. "I assume you have never driven in a motor vehicle before," he asked as he put Assad's suitcase in the back. "Well, hop in. You are in for a treat."

Although many of the roads leading to Downtown Camden were not as of yet paved, and the journey was a little bumpy in spots, Assad thoroughly enjoyed the ride. "I would like to buy one for Frances someday," he thought to himself.

"You'll stay at my place tonight—my wife is visiting her sister for a week in Philadelphia—and in the morning I'll run you over to the Campbell Soup Factory. It's quite a place." Nabih continued, "You can stay with us until you find an apartment of your own."

"Thank you, Nabih," Assad said, feeling slightly embarrassed. "You have done more than is necessary." Nabih took one hand off the wheel and waved it dismissively. The car involuntarily swerved. Nabih quickly returned both hands to the wheel. "Nonsense, what is family for." He suddenly pointed off to the left. "Look over there!" Looking off to his right, Assad could see dozens of small factory buildings, but several caught his eye as they had what looked like large cans of soup on a tripod, towering above the buildings.

"That's the Campbell Soup Factory," said Nabih. "It's one of the fastest growing companies in all of the United States. That's where you'll be working. Lots of Italians. It'll feel like home. Do you like soup?"

As they got closer to Nabih's tenement, Assad could see that Camden was in the midst of a growth spurt. Four and five-story buildings dotted the roads and there were a number of small shops and the occasional good-sized department store. And a movie theatre; Assad had never seen a motion picture as they were a fairly new phenomena in America. The population on the streets appeared to be a mixture of white and black faces, some smartly dressed and others rather shabbily. There were a great number of automobiles traveling along the street as a tribute to progress, but also a fairly good number of horse-drawn wagons, perhaps in a tribute to tradition. They seemed to live in some kind of harmony, with only the occasional honking of a horn.

Nabih's apartment was on the third floor of a four-story tenement. As Assad took the stairs each landing offered a barrage of both cooking smells and languages. Assad detected Italian, of course, plus German and Spanish; maybe even a little Arabic.

Upon entering the apartment Assad could not help but notice how neat and orderly it was. Nabih noticed the look on Assad's face and said, "Trust me, I am not this neat. But my wife—God bless her—is incredibly neat. And I don't dare mess it up while she is gone. There's a spare bedroom off to your right; put your bag in there."

Assad did as he was told and when he returned he found Nabih standing near the table holding out a bottle of beer to him. "To a new beginning," offered Nabih. Assad took the beer, clinked bottles and drank. It tasted delicious.

Nabih wiped the foam from his lips. "When do you envision your family arriving?" he asked. "Can I assume after the winter has passed?" Assad nodded. "Yes," he replied. "Most likely April or May; I will write them once I am settled in a job."

"Sounds like a good plan," Nabih concurred. "The timing might also work out well for you. I am told by the landlord that there may be an empty apartment coming available in April. It's on the first floor."

Assad's face lit up with the news, as he had been stressed on what it would take to find housing. "I plan on writing Frances right after I start the new job; I will tell her then. She'll be very happy, as will the children."

Nabih snapped his fingers and put the bottle down on the table. He hurried over to the refrigerator and reached for a piece of paper on top. "Speaking of the job, here is the information you will need tomorrow morning when you get there." He handed the letter to Assad, who looked at it intently. "Terry McClusky." Assad looked at Nabih. "He is the supervisor?"

"Yes, a real good guy, but a little rough around the edges, so to speak. His wife and mine are friends from the Women's Auxiliary. Like I said he's gruff but has a good heart."

Assad put the letter in his jacket pocket. "Okay, I will see him tomorrow."

"Oh, and Assad..." Assad looked up at Nabih. "Don't get offended." Assad was confused. "Why would I get offended?"

Nabih looked down at his feet, almost embarrassed. "Like I said, Terry is a good guy. But he's very... what's the word?... 'Colorful'. But as I mentioned," Nabih stressed, "A very good guy."

At that point, Assad wasn't sure what to expect.

"Jesus wept! Not another wop!"

Assad was slightly taken aback by the comments from the ruddy-looking individual sitting behind a large wooden desk. He was stocky, with a red face, puffy cheeks, and a nose that appeared to be spider-webbed with veins. His hair was grey and bushy. His chest thick, with suspenders over his shirt, the sleeves rolled up to the elbow to reveal muscular arms adorned with numerous tattoos. But for whatever reason, or perhaps because he had been forewarned by Nabih, the words came out of the man's mouth with a complete lack of venom.

"It's not bad enough I have to put up with polacks, krauts, Arabs, spics... now I have more wops. Jesus wept!"

"Actually, sir, I am not Italian. I was born in Leb..."

"I don't give a rat's ass which god-forsaken country your mother squirted you out," the man interrupted."You look Italian…" The supervisor, Terry McClusky, looked down again at the letter Assad had handed him." "ASS-ad… sounds wop, to me." At that point Assad thought it wise not to contradict.

"So, ASS-ad," McClusky said, reaching into a bottom drawer and pulling out a bottle of whiskey which he placed on his desk. "Do you have any particular skills we can use here?"

"Well," Assad answered. "Back in Argentina and Italy I used to be a jeweler." McClusky poured some of the whisky into a dusty metal cup. "A jeweler…great. If we decide to invent Diamond Soup you are first on my list to call. What else ya got? C'mon, give me something to work with." Assad wasn't sure what else to say, so McClusky answered for him.

"So what are you, six-feet two, maybe three?"

"I think so."

"In pretty good shape, are ya?"

"I am not afraid of manual labor."

"Good," McClusky answered, gulping down the cup of whiskey in one large gulp. "Because we have plenty of manual labor to do around here." He rose from the chair and grabbed his sweater. "I think loading trucks might be just perfect for you. C'mon, I'll introduce you to the foreman on the loading dock. His name is Richter. I think maybe he's German. Who the hell knows?" They both started for the door but then McClusky stopped abruptly and Assad almost ran into his back. The supervisor turned and said, "You don't hate krauts, do ya?"

Assad thought for a moment and then replied, "I don't know... I never met one." McClusky smiled. "Good answer. C'mon, let's go meet your first kraut. It'll be fun."

As Assad and McClusky made their way through the factory Assad was amazed at the amount of work being done. There were long lines of women in long dresses putting labels on cans and placing them in boxes, where young men would tape them up and get them ready for shipping. It was like watching a well-oiled machine.

Finally both men exited the factory onto the loading dock where Assad could see at least a dozen horse and wagons ready to be loaded, each with the words 'Joseph Campbell Company' emblazoned on the side. Obviously the transportation progress being seen on the streets hadn't touched the Campbell Soup Company as of yet, as Mr. Joseph Campbell still preferred the old-fashioned way of moving his soup around the country.

"There he is," McClusky bellowed, pointing to the far end of the dock. "Hey Richter! Got somebody for you to meet."

The man wiped his brow and started walking toward McClusky. He was young and muscular, with jet black hair and long sideburns. His strides were long and purposeful. "What are you shouting about, you dumb mick?"

"Richter, meet your new hire. This here is ASS-ad."

Assad put out his hand and tried not to wince in Richter's powerful grip. "Assad Hajjar." The German smiled. "Klaus Richter. Welcome aboard."

McClusky grinned. "How touching; a friendship between Germany and Italy." Assad attempted again to correct him. "I told you, I'm not…."

"Yeah, whatever," McClusky replied as he turned and walked away. "He's all yours Richter."

Assad stared at McClusky's back as he walked back into the factory. "That is the strangest man…"

Richter laughed. "Don't let the big lug get to you; he's really a teddy bear." Assad found it hard to believe the description. "He is?"

"Sure. Let me tell you a story; and don't ever repeat that I told it to you." Richter looked around as if every ear in the factory was waiting on his next words. He dropped his voice a notch.

"About six months ago this young Spanish kid was loading heavy boxes and slipped. His hand got caught between the boxes and the end of the truck and smashed just about every bone in his hand. God, it was awful," Richter looked around again. "So the kid can't work, right? I mean, he's got a busted hand and all. And he's got a wife and two little kids. So McClusky not only pays for the kid's hospitalization, he delivered a whole basketful of food to the family. Keeps it all on the hush-hush, less everyone think he's one of the good guys, you know?"

Assad was shocked. "He did all that?"

"Yup, sure did." Assad just shook his head.

"Now c'mon… I'll show you what we do around here."

CHAPTER ELEVEN

April 1915

Buenos Aires, Argentina

January 12, 1915
From: Assad Hajjar
Camden, New Jersey, USA

My Dearest Frances,

Words cannot describe how much I have missed you all these months. It was especially hard at Christmastime—I hope you received the presents I shipped to you for the children.

Nabih and his wife did everything to make me feel like part of their family during the holidays. But there was always a hole in my heart.

The job at the Campbell Soup Factory is going well. The work is hard and the pay okay. But the people are very nice and I've made a few friends along the way. I have secured us a small apartment in the building where Nabih lives. It's not a palace but I believe you will find it adequate. The other tenants are hardworking people and I think you will like them.

Nabih has shared with me that I also have relatives in Massachusetts, just south of Boston. Perhaps we will get to visit them someday.

But for now I wish you a safe and uneventful journey. I count the days until we are together, all of us, once again, as a family.

Travel safe and hug the children for me. I will see you soon. In America.

Your loving husband, Assad

Frances read the letter one more time before putting it in her coat pocket. She continued to pack clothes into the suitcase that lay open on the bed. She knew the children were in their rooms, also packing for the trip.

"What's this, Momma?" asked 6-year old Lydia, her fingers tracing the outline of the item resting on a blanket on the bed. "It's beautiful."

Frances smiled and gripped her daughter's shoulders softly. "That, Lydia, is what is referred to as a Holy Relic. It was given to your father by the Pope himself. In Rome."

"What's a Pope," she asks innocently, her eyes still fixed on the item on the bed. Frances could only smile as she answered.

"The Pope is like God on earth," said Frances. "He is very powerful. He gave that to your Poppa for all the good work he had done when we were living in Italy."

Frances pointed at the Holy Relic. "You see, here is an actual piece of wood from the cross that Jesus Christ died on. And these are pieces of bones from holy men." With that Lydia wrinkled her nose. *"Ewwww."*

Frances smiled at her daughter. "The Pope told us we can never sell this to anyone, and we must always keep it in our family. Perhaps someday it will be yours, then you will hand it down to your children." Lydia nodded.

Khalil, now 15-years old and looking more and more like his father, leaned into the room from the doorway. "Momma, the taxi is here to take us to the pier." With that Frances wrapped the Holy Relic securely in a thick blanket and placed it between her clothes in the suitcase. She then secured the suitcase and handed it to Khalil. "Thank you. I'll be right out." Khalil exited the room, followed by Lydia close on his heels. Frances could hear Lydia's voice as she walked down the hall. "Khalil, did you ever hear of this Pope man?"

Frances took one more look around the room. It saddened her that once again she was leaving her home. But that sadness was tempered by the excitement of a new life, and seeing Assad again. It was also Assad that made the decision that he would travel to America first, in steerage, in order to save enough money so that Frances and the children could undertake the long voyage from Argentina in comfort, with their own cabin.

She took the letter she had written for Beca and placed it on the nightstand. Turned off the light and left the darkened room.

The voyage to New York had taken a little over two weeks and the children actually enjoyed themselves. The captain even offered to take them on a tour, which delighted them all. Khalil was engrossed in the history of the vessel, and 13-year-old Tecla was engrossed in the good-looking second-mate. The first-class accommodations also offered the opportunity to pass through the immigration process with relative ease, although Frances was saddened to see so many poor immigrants, all carrying no more than a battered suitcase, the clothes on their back, and a hope for a better life.

As Assad instructed, they had taken the small ferry across to New Jersey and now waited for him just beyond the dock, taking in the shade offered by a large oak tree on this unusually warm May afternoon. They turned their attention to a honking horn and were all surprised at what they saw.

"Frances!" yelled Assad from the front seat of Nabih's motor vehicle, waving his arm frantically. "Frances!"

"Momma, what is father driving?" asked Tecla. Before Frances could answer her daughter, Assad had stopped the automobile and was vaulting out of the front seat. He engulfed his wife in his strong arms. "I missed you so much... and the children." They all ran to hug him.

"We missed you as well, husband... but what is *that*?" she asked, pointing at the car. Assad proudly pointed at the idling automobile. "That is Nabih's automobile. He taught me how to drive it!" Frances looked skeptical. "And we can all fit in there?"

Assad grabbed the luggage from the children and placed them in a compartment at the back of the car. "Sure, no problem," he beamed. "You will sit in the front seat with me with Lydia on your lap. And Tecla, Inez and Khalil will sit in the back. See? Plenty of room!"

And with that they all piled into Nabih's automobile; which was a snug fit but surprisingly comfortable. "And we're off!" Assad proclaimed, giving the horn a last toot for good measure.

Camden, NJ in the summer of 1915 is hot and sticky. At times the heat coming off the sidewalk is unbearable. But although their small first-floor apartment is hot, there would occasionally be a breeze coming through a side window.

Assad was working six days a week, 10-hours a day at the Campbell Soup Factory, and Frances was earning a little extra money doing some light tutoring for some of the neighbor's children. Khalil, Tecla, Inez, even Lydia, had made friends with kids in their own age group, several who would suddenly pop over for dinner on any given night. Frances was more than happy to cook for them. She had also enjoyed the company of Nabih and his wife, Sophia. And since they had no children of their own they immediately took to Frances' own children.

Perhaps Frances' closest friends were her next-door neighbor, a black family that had recently made the move to the United States from Jamaica. The husband also worked at the Campbell Soup Factory, so the wife, Josslin, was often left home alone with their five-year-old daughter, Mercy. She was a delightful child and Lydia played with her often.

It was the usual sweltering afternoon in mid-August and Frances was fanning herself with a magazine with one hand while stirring a big pot of spaghetti sauce with the other. The silence was broken by Lydia's shrill scream. "Momma, come quick… something is wrong with Mercy!"

Frances immediately turned off the stove and rushed out into the hallway where she saw Lydia standing in Jocelyn's doorway, crying. "Hurry!" Frances hurtled past Lydia where she saw Mercy lying on the sofa, crying out in pain while she clutched her stomach. Her mother stood off to the side, crying. "Frances… I don't know what to do… I don't know what is wrong!"

Frances moved quickly to the child's side and pressed gently on her lower abdomen. The child arched in pain and screamed. Frances stood up and took Josslin by the shoulders. "Listen to me. Her appendix has burst, and she will die if we don't get her to a hospital." With that news Josslin's eyes widened. "But… but… the hospital is over a mile away. How will we get her there? We don't have a car or a wagon…" She started to wail uncontrollably.

"LISTEN TO ME, Josslin!" The mother stopped crying and stared at Frances. "We have to get Mercy to the hospital, as fast as possible." With that Frances looked frantically around the room. "Do you still have her baby carriage?" Josslin stared at her as if she had asked her what the formula was to make rocket fuel. "JOSSLIN! Do … you... have… a… baby carriage?"

"There's one in the bedroom," offered Lydia. "Good," Frances answered. "Go get it, Lydia." She looked at Josslin, "Wrap Mercy in a blanket and put her in the carriage." Josslin didn't move. "NOW!" She did as she was instructed.

To the average person on the street, now desperately trying to avoid being hit by a baby carriage being pushed frantically by a middle-aged woman, it probably seemed surreal. But for Frances Ersillia Hajjar, with nothing in front of her but Cooper Hospital just over a mile away, it was a mission of mercy. Frances' back was soaked from the heat of the hot August sun and sweat dripped from her hands as they tightly held the carriage handles. Mercy's screams didn't help as they hit bump after bump, but Frances could hardly blame her; the girl was in severe pain.

Knowing that Josslin and Lydia could never keep up with her pace, she left them tasked with tracking down Josslin's husband and having them all meet at the hospital. Moving as fast as she could, her legs now starting to slightly cramp, Frances could see the front door of the hospital in the distance. Giving it all she had, she kicked into another burst of energy and soon she was pushing the carriage with the wailing child into the reception area, amidst the stares of several patients sitting in chairs waiting to be seen.

Behind the glass a middle-aged woman sat talking on a telephone, seemingly ignoring Frances's' frantic gestures. Frustrated Frances knocked on the glass. "Hello, this child has a burst appendix... she needs to be seen by a doctor at once!"

The woman's reply, delivered with an air of impatience was simply, "I'm sorry, you'll have to take a seat. Someone will be with you shortly." And with that she went back to talking on the phone, ignoring Frances. A big mistake.

With one smooth gesture and all the strength she could muster, Frances grabbed an ashtray stand and swung it with all her might against the glass. The receptionist practically fell out of her chair and several people leaped from their seats. As Frances wound up for another swing, her aim was put on hold by a hand grabbing her arm.

"I don't think we will need another wake-up call," said a voice, surprisingly pleasant in lieu of the turmoil unfolding. "I think you have our attention."

Frances put down the ashtray and looked at the doctor, who was young and blond-haired, perhaps all of 25. "I am Dr. Corkins. How can I assist you?" Frances leaned over and tried to catch her breath, the adrenaline now starting to ooze from her body. "This child... appendix... burst, I think. Needs help." she said between breathes that were hard to come by.

Dr. Corkins looked at the child and his face turned serious. "Orderly... a stretcher...NOW!" he yelled. Immediately a stretcher appeared and a moaning Mercy was put on it and wheeled through large double doors. The doctor turned to Frances, "Don't worry; we'll take care of her."

"Thank you," said Frances. It was the last thing she remembered saying before hitting the floor hard.

"Frances, Frances... are you okay?"

Assad was relieved to see his wife's eyes slowly open and the color on her cheeks begin to return. She was seated in a chair in the waiting room. In front of her stood Assad, Josslin's husband, Carlito, and Lydia, who looked very frightened. She stroked Lydia's hair, "I'm fine. What happened?"

Assad answered, "The doctor said you passed out, probably from running a mile in 90-degree heat pushing a baby carriage."

"In order to save my daughter's life," Josslin's husband, Carlito interjected. "How can I ever thank you?"

"Mercy?" Frances asked.

"She is in surgery, but the doctor thinks she will be fine," said Carlito, bending down to kiss Frances' hand, who was embarrassed by the sweet gesture. "That makes me happy," she replied.

Assad helped Frances to her feet. "Carlito will stay with his wife and daughter," said Assad. "Come, we will go home now."

Frances smiled as she stood and took a second to regain her balance. "Good idea," she said. "I left some sauce on the stove."

For the next year or so, Frances was treated as a celebrity by all her neighbors for her heroics in saving the child's life. The local paper had even done a feature story on her, which included a photo of a smiling Frances and Mercy hugging.

It was March of 1916 and Assad was hoisting perhaps his one hundredth carton of soup cans on the back of a truck while the driver stood off to the side leisurely reading the latest issue of *Leslie's Monthly Magazine.* Assad put the carton in its place and arched his back, hearing the tendons crackle.

"Assad! Telephone," Klaus yelled from the other side of the dock. He looked up to see his friend holding out the receiver. "For me?" Assad asked sheepishly, knowing he knew no one in Camden who owned a phone. Even Nabih had yet to purchase this relatively new invention. "Do you know who it is?" he asked, wiping his brow and walking towards Klaus. "Nah," came the response. "But they said they were calling from somewhere near Boston. The line is a little crackly." He handed the receiver to a confused looking Assad, who took it in his hands like it was radioactive. He put the receiver up to his ear and spoke into the mouthpiece.

"Hello?" he said hesitantly. The voice on the other end, although as Klaus had said was a little static-filled, was that of a woman and she spoke fairly loud and perfectly clear.

"Is this Assad Hajjar?"

"Yes, it is. May I ask to whom I am speaking?" His question was answered by a soft chuckle. "Of course you may," came the reply. "My name is Zaina Khoury... well it used to be Zaina Hajjar. Nabih is my second-cousin."

Assad smiled. "Another cousin? It seems to me like our family is quite larger than I anticipated. How are you, Zaina?"

Zaina laughed a hearty laugh. "I am quite well, cousin. And congratulations on marrying what can only be described as a remarkable woman!" Although Assad and Frances had not been legally married, Assad discovered long ago it was much easier just to avoid the implication. "I assume you are talking about saving our neighbor's child's life… yes that was something."

"I would say so," Zaina agreed. "Nabih sent me the newspaper article. It was a wonderful write-up."

"Thank you, Zaina," Assad said. "But I am guessing you are not calling from as far away as Boston just to talk about a newspaper story." Again, Assad was greeted by a boisterous laugh. Although Assad had yet to meet Zaina, he was already taken in by her infectious spirit.

"You got that right, Assad. Actually, I am calling to see if you would be interested in moving your family up to Massachusetts?" Assad was stunned by the offer, as it wasn't remotely what he expected this phone call to be about.

"Massachusetts?" was all he could manage to reply.

"Jesus, Mary and Joseph, you make it sound like I asked you to move to the moon," came Zaina's response. "We are in a beautiful area just south of Boston, with sidewalks lined with trees and some wonderful rivers and mountains, which I think your wife and children would thoroughly enjoy more than Camden, no offense to Nabih. And we have two new wonderful schools opening up in September for the children. Assad, I am offering you roots."

"It's not that, it's... well where would we live... what would I do for work?"

"Well, as fate would have it we have a house that we were renting out to a young couple but they decided to move back to Portugal, so we could rent that to you. As for work, my husband's brother is one of the supervisors at the Slater and Morrill Shoe Company in Braintree, MA, and I am told there is an opening for a loading dock foreman."

Assad's mind was reeling from the conversation, but he had to admit he was excited. "I would have to talk with Frances about moving again," Assad said.

"I understand," answered Zaina. "I will wait to hear from you. And Assad...."

"Yes?"

"Don't wait too long to get back to me; I can't be certain how long the job will be available."

"I understand and thank you Zaina for reaching out. Perhaps we will see each other soon?"

"I hope so," came the reply, followed by the laugh that was starting to grow on Assad. "Family should always be together."

CHAPTER TWELVE

April 1916

Braintree, Massachusetts

The time spent in Camden, New Jersey wasn't especially long, but it was meaningful. Frances' heroics, even a year later, were still spoken of in revered tones by all the neighbors, and when Assad and his family boarded the New York, New Haven and Hartford Railroad train at Camden destined for Boston's South Station, it was a sendoff for the ages. Hundreds of people gathered at the terminal to bid them farewell, a sight that the children talked about for most of the five-hour journey north.

The family was in good spirits; the children suddenly feeling like maybe they had found roots for the first time after jumping from continent to continent, and Frances looking chipper. She held Assad's hand for most of the way. She was looking forward to seeing the house.

During the trip, as the train made its way north through towns with names like New Haven, Bridgeport and Stamford, Assad did some reading up on his future employer, information that had been sent to him by Zaina. According to the literature in his possession, the Slater and Morrill Shoe Company, located on Pearl Street in Braintree, MA, had been around for decades and had established itself as one of the nation's leading manufacturers of footwear. The building itself, which Assad observed in a photo attached to the information, was a very long non-descript four-story building, the type you would see in any large city. Either way, Assad was looking forward to starting. He had never shied away from hard work.

Assad looked down at the seat beside him and noticed a copy of *The Boston American*, a newspaper someone had likely left from the previous trip. It was face down but the back page had a headline in thick black type: **Mayor Curley To Throw Out First Pitch at Red Sox Home Opener Against the Athletics.**

Assad had heard about this American game that had steadily grown in popularity since the turn of the century. Perhaps, as a new American, he should start showing more interest, perhaps even secure tickets and take Khalil to a game at Fenway Park.

"SOUTH STATION!"

With the announcement by the conductor, Assad told the children to start packing up their books and games. They did as they were told and soon the six of them were standing in the middle of Boston's South Station, a huge concourse with massive pillars and a glass ceiling that seemed to go on forever. They were all in awe, and only came back to reality upon hearing the thundering voice of Zaina Khoury.

"You must be Assad and Frances!" boomed the small but portly woman who now came barreling toward them. Frances barely had time to react before she was engulfed in a bear hug that nearly took her breath way. She smiled sheepishly at Assad while the children all laughed. "It is so nice to finally meet all of you!"

Assad extended his hand, which Zaina folded into both of hers. "We can't thank you enough for this great opportunity," he said. "We are so very happy to be here."

"The pleasure is ours," she replied quickly. "Come, you must be tired. My husband, Izzy, is waiting outside with the car. It's about a 20-minute drive south of the city to your new home."

The drive was pleasant enough with the children in awe of the many cars and buildings throughout Boston, which was no doubt a booming metropolis. Izzy was a pleasant fellow, though at a height close to six feet and no more than 160 pounds on his frame, he was rail-thin and offered quite a contrast to his rather hefty wife. And Zaina was correct, once the car exited the city there were more and more tree-lined streets and single-family homes.

"Look on your left, Assad... that is the Slater and Morrill Shoe Factory." Assad glanced over to where Zaina was pointing to see a building that pretty much looked like the photo. "Izzy's brother, Dmitri, will meet you there on Monday morning, so you have the weekend to get settled in your new home."

Assad could only smile, feeling Frances' hand tighten in his.

"Here we go—Crescent Street—and your new home," proclaimed Zaina as she pointed out to her husband an empty parking space in front of a small but charming white clapboard home. Zaina jumped out first—Assad was amazed at how quickly she could move for a big woman—and with an air of pomp and circumstance, opened the door to the car and bowed, "Mr. and Mrs. Assad Hajjar... *welcome home!"*

It was Tuesday, September 4, 1917 and Assad had to admit the past year couldn't have gone by any smoother. Frances quickly made the house her own and would constantly invite the neighbors over for tea and general gossip. Khalil, now 17, and Tecla, who just turned 15 had started high school in Braintree and made friends already. And Inez, 12, and Lydia, all of 8, were still getting used to their respective schools. Meanwhile, the job at the shoe factory turned out to be the perfect fit for Assad, who quickly became a favorite of all the workers thanks to his wit and charm, which were always on display. As matter of fact it was Assad managing to be in the good graces of his supervisor that enable him and Khalil to be sitting in choice seats on the third base side of Fenway Park on this warm Tuesday afternoon, enjoying a game between the Red Sox and the New York Yankees.

Khalil appeared to enjoy himself immensely, and Assad wasn't surprised because it took no time for his son to abandon his love of soccer for this great American pastime. If there was any damper to be on display this afternoon, it was Assad's observation that between munching on hot dogs and gulping down Cracker Jack, his son seemed to be coughing and sniffling a little more than usual. But Assad quickly dismissed it as perhaps allergies. The Red Sox were up 4-2 as the Yankees came to bat.

"Poppa, have you ever seen anyone pitch so great? I can't believe how almost no one can seem to hit him." Assad could see his son staring intently at the portly figure on the mound wearing the "B" on his cap. "I mean, he doesn't even seem to be in that good a shape; kind of fat, actually. What's his name again?"

Assad scanned his program. "It says here... *Babe Ruth.* Strange name. But you are right, Khalil, he does seem a bit out of shape. I wouldn't be surprised if this is his last good game he plays." Khalil smiled at his father's comments, before suddenly going into a body-wracking fit of coughing. Assad felt it was time to leave.

Khalil started to feel a little better over the holidays, even to the point of helping other families that also seemed to be dealing deal with this terrible illness. But by early-February of 1918 his own symptoms worsened; the cough was getting more violent and he was having trouble breathing, plus strange marks were appearing on his skin. Doctors were concerned because news had started to surface about troops fighting in the war that might be bringing something infectious with them on their journey home. And by the spring of that year, the medical community had given it a name... The Spanish Flu.

Once the Spanish Flu erupted it seemed on an unstoppable path. Hospitals filled up at an alarming rate and people, now in full panic, stayed in their houses and only ventured out if truly needed, then while wearing a face covering. As the death toll started to climb, particularly among young people, the economy snapped like a dry twig. Businesses closed down, movie theatres stopped showing films, sporting events ceased.

Assad's situation was a reflection of the pandemic. One day he went late into the shoe factory only to find rows of empty desks which normally would have been ablaze with activity. The situation on the factory floor was just as bad. The first thing Assad noticed when he walked out of the elevator was the silence. No machines were running. No one was around, except for his supervisor, sitting on a barrel smoking a cigarette. Assad could even see trucks filled with shoes sitting at the loading docks, with obviously nowhere to go.

"Gerry, what's going on?" Assad asked looking around. The man flicked the ashes of his cigarette on the floor. "The boss sent everyone home, what's the point? People aren't going out to buy shoes, so the shoe stores have full shelves. So if their shelves are full, why do they need more shoes delivered... get it?" Assad did, and it made him feel even sadder.

In late-May of 1918, The Spanish Flu picked up deadly speed and indiscriminately lay waste to countless millions across the United States... including 18-year old Khalil Hajjar.

Needless to say, Frances was devastated by the loss of her only son and would suddenly break into fits of hysteria without warning. It seemed to push her fragile mental state to the brink. Following Khalil's death she made Tecla, Lydia and Inez wear—much to their horror—only black clothes to school. The meaner classmates dubbed them "The Black Crow Sisters." Assad feared this might be the one tragedy his wife may not recover from. He prayed that wouldn't be so.

On a rainy night a few weeks after Khalil was buried in a cemetery in Quincy, MA, Assad awoke to find that Frances was no longer beside him in the bed. His watch said 11:30pm. Thunder crashed outside the window. Assad searched the house and found only his children asleep in their rooms. He went down to the kitchen, hoping to find Frances there. But all he found was a note on the table, in Frances' handwriting.

"I remember when Khalil was a small boy. Whenever it would rain hard and there was thunder and lightning he would get so scared. His fear would only go away if I slept beside him. Then he would truly be at peace."

Assad crumpled the note in his hand and grabbed his raincoat from the coat rack. He quickly ran out the back door and jumped into his car. A bolt of lightning illuminated the street in front of him.

Assad entered the Mount Wollaston Cemetery off Rte 3A, across from Greenleaf Street. He knew exactly where he was going as two weeks ago he buried his son there. The rain came down harder. Although it was dark, a burst of lightning provided enough illumination to see the sad figure of Frances Assad, lying on the stone that served as the final resting place of her only son. She wore her pajamas and bathrobe, now soaked and clinging to her skin.

Assad got out of the car and walked slowly over to his wife. "Frances?" She looked slowly up at him and smiled, but her gaze seemed far away. "Assad, you've come to help keep him safe." His heart ached. "He is safe, my love." He helped her to her feet and he could feel her shiver. "Come, we have to go home." She looked down at the stone and up at the rain which washed across her face. "But who will keep him warm and safe?"

Assad took off his raincoat and placed it over the stone. "There, now he will be dry," he said softly, leading his wife back to the car. She stopped just before getting into the car and faced Assad, asking a question that would tear at his heart forever.

"Assad, why does God hate me? Did I do something wrong? Can you tell him..." She looked once more at Khalil's grave. "... that I am sorry?"

CHAPTER 13

January 1920

Boston, Massachusetts

The snow fell heavily and at a steady pace as Assad sat alone in a wooden booth of the Union Oyster House in Downtown Boston. He checked his watch and saw that the man he was meeting there—a friend from work—was a few minutes late, but paid it no mind. Weather had a way of playing havoc with schedules.

As Assad looked out the window he thought back on the past two years, to what had transpired, both for the good and for the bad. The tragic death of his son, Khalil, and his mother's subsequent breakdown were in a whole category of bad by itself. But Assad had seen some positive steps with Frances, mostly thanks to her involvement in some women's issues, which was the very elixir that saved her from depression back in Argentina. Her strong will and fierce determination made her a natural when it came to battling social injustice. He admired her for that.

The girls weren't doing as well. Tecla was set to graduate from high school in the spring but dropped out because of the constant harassment she received from classmates for constantly wearing black clothes, per Frances' instructions. She was now working at a restaurant near the Quincy shipyard, owned by a second cousin of Zaina. Apparently there were Hajjars everywhere. Sadly, Inez followed in her sister's footsteps and also refused to go to school.

The door of the bar opened and Assad looked up to see his co-worker at the shoe company, Dominic Luchessi, walking in as he brushed the show off his coat sleeves. He was not alone. With him was a tall man, heavily built with a bushy mustache. He wore a cap worn low over his brow.

"Hey Assad, sorry I'm late," offered Dominic. Assad rose to shake his friend's hand. "And I'd like you to meet a friend of mind, who I just happened to run into and I asked him to join us." Dominic made the introductions; "Assad Hajjar, meet Bartolomeo Vanzetti… Bartolomeo, this is Assad Hajjar. He isn't Italian … but we don't hold that against him because he married a beautiful Italian woman from Messina." Both men shook hands and all three once again sat down in the booth.

"Assad works with me at the Slater and Morrill Shoe Company," Dominic said to Vanzetti, and Assad couldn't help but notice a slight twitch in his eye upon mentioning the shoe company. "Bartolomeo here is kind of between jobs, but working for a fish company down in Plymouth... that right?" Vanzetti nodded and took a sip of the beer that had been placed in front of him by a waitress. "I am kind of between jobs at the moment; just trying to keep busy," Vanzetti offered, looking down at his beer.

Dominic slapped him on the back, "Don't worry, something will come up." He pulls out his watch, "Shit, I have to go, sorry." He gulps down the remainder of his beer. "But you guys hang out, get to know each other." With that Dominic Luchessi was out the door in a flash.

Turns out that for the next two hours Assad and Bartolomeo did get to share some information. What Assad learned from his new friend was that Vanzetti was a bachelor and a bit of a wandering free spirit. He was 32-years old and immigrated to the U.S. in 1908 from Villafalletto, a region in Northern Italy not far from Turin. He worked for a short spell as a kitchen helper in New York, then at various small jobs in the Boston area. He also spent some time in Mexico. He appeared to be very soft-spoken and reserved, and only showed some interest when Assad mentioned Frances' work on behalf of workers in Argentina.

"I would very much like to meet this strong woman," Vanzetti says. "I already admire her very much for the good work she has done and continues to do." Assad thanks him for the kind words and then makes a bold suggestion. "Bartolomeo, you mentioned you live by yourself. In that case, why not join us for dinner on Saturday evening? I am sure you would enjoy some homemade Italian cooking." Vanzetti appeared stunned by the offer; as if it were the first time someone showed him a kindness. "It would be my honor," he acknowledges with a small bow of his head.

Assad jots his address down on the back of a napkin and slides it over. "Let's say 6pm?" Bartolomeo Vanzetti smiles. "I look forward to it." He glances at his own watch. "But now I must go," he explains standing. "I have to meet another friend.

But I will see you on Saturday." With that he again bows, turned, and exits the restaurant.

When Assad promised Bartolomeo some real Italian cooking, he wasn't kidding. When Assad first told Frances they would be having a guest for dinner on Saturday night, her reaction was one of weary boredom, a trait she had been displaying quite often since Khalil's passing. But upon mentioning that guest was from her homeland, and also a recent visitor to their new country, her attention span ratcheted up quite a few notches. She went into full Italian hostess mode.

The kitchen table was filled with pasta, meatballs, sausages, gnocchi and salad. As Frances stood there admiring her presentation, there came a knock on the door. Assad opened the door to find Bartolomeo standing there; flowers in one hand, a bottle of wine in the other. "Come in, come in," says Assad. "Please meet my... wife; Frances Ersillia Galliotti Hajjar. Frances, this is Bartolomeo Vanzetti."

With that Bartolomeo hands off the flowers and wine to Assad and crossed the room to Frances. He removes his hat and kisses her hand. "Signora, it is my great pleasure." And with that Frances goes into full blush mode. "Please, it is so nice you can join us. Assad, please open the wine and I will find a vase for the beautiful flowers. Then we can eat." She looks at Bartolomeo and said, "I hope you are hungry?" He returns her question with a smile, "Like a bear."

The meal is delightful and after the table has been cleared and coffee poured, the talk continues. Most of the conversation centers on the various regions of Italy; Bartolomeo's home in the north, and Frances' in the south. She tells him of her father's bravery and mentions that she had actually met Pope Pius, but did not go into detail the circumstances of the meeting; Assad never confided to their guest that he was a priest.

At some point the conversation did turn to Frances' work with the women's movement in Argentina, which Bartolomeo greatly admired. "I have always felt the need to fight for those who are being held down by governments, no matter where that government might be," he stresses. "I have a friend who came over with me from Italy, his name is Nicola, and he once introduced me to a man named Luigi Galleani, who has advocated the need to help those in need."

"Galleani? Isn't he the one the newspapers are calling an anarchist?" Assad asks. Bartolomeo waves his hand

179

dismissively. "Rubbish! Those are just labels the media places on people whose ideas they either don't understand or don't believe in." He turns to Frances. "Believe me, Frances, I would do *anything* to bring about change, but it would never inspire me to use violence or harm someone. You believe that, don't you?" Frances nods her head slowly, "I do." With that Bartolomeo lets loose a hearty laugh. "Excellent! Now, is that a tiramisu I see over there on the counter?"

The afternoon of Thursday, April 15, 1920 was cool but with the promise of temperatures warming up to nearly 60 degrees, a welcome respite from what had been a cold snowy winter in the Boston area. Assad had agreed to work the second shift that day, starting at 4pm and running until midnight. It was just after 3:30pm when he took the corner onto Pearl Street in South Braintree; where the Slater and Morrill Shoe Company was located, and he knew right way it wasn't going to be a normal day.

In front of the building there had to be at least a half-dozen Braintree police wagons and perhaps two ambulances. People were milling about. Assad pulled his car into the parking lot. He got out and surveyed the scene. He saw Dominic talking with one of the police officers. As he walked over he saw Dominic being thanked by the officer, who then shut his notebook and walked away. "Dominic... what the hell is going on?"

Dominic turned and acknowledged Assad with a nod. "It's pretty bad, Assad. "There was a robbery... and a killing." Assad was stunned. "What robbery... who was killed?"

Dominic took a deep breath and took out a cigarette. He lit the cigarette, took a long drag, and exhaled the smoke slowly.

"According to what the police are saying, two men were robbed and killed while transporting the Slater and Morrill's payroll to the main factory, just over $15,000." Dominic took another puff. "One of them was a security guard, Alessandro Berardelli. Did you know him?" Assad shook his head no. "He was shot four times; never got his revolver out of his holster. Then they shot the paymaster, Frederick Parmenter." Assad knew that name.

"Freddy got shot! I just had lunch with him a few days ago... is he alright?" Dominic shook his head as he stubbed out the cigarette he had tossed on the ground. "No, he's dead. But I guess as this was all happening, a car with some other men pulled up and just starting shooting wildly. Fortunately, no one was hit."

Assad couldn't believe what he was hearing. "Do the police have any idea who might have done this terrible thing?" Dominic just shrugged his shoulder and pulled his cap down tighter on his head. "They say they do... but who knows?" As Dominic started to walk away he yelled over his shoulder to Assad, "But I tell you, when they do catch those guys, I wouldn't want to be in their shoes."

In the little over a week that passed since the robbery and murders, Assad only heard snippets on the radio and in the newspapers about whatever progress was being made by the authorities. By all reports a person of interest was a man named Ferruccio Coacci, who was being labeled in the newspaper as an anarchist (Assad thought back to the last time he heard that word used; right here in this very kitchen). It was also reported that the car used in the crime was found abandoned. But from what Assad could ascertain, the police still had no real suspects on their radar. At least that's what Assad thought, until there was a knock on his door the evening of April 23, 1920.

"Yes, who is it?"

"Assad Hajjar?"

"Who is asking?"

"We are with the Braintree Police Department. Can you open the door, sir?" Like most immigrants, Assad had an embedded fear of the police. "What's this all about?"

"Please sir. Open the door." Knowing he had no choice, Assad opens the door to see two men, in suits, holding out wallets with badges in them. One man is tall and thin, with thick red hair. The other is shorter, stockier, and completely bald. But he has mean eyes and a face that looked like it was glued in a permanent sneer. The stub of an unlit cigar hangs from the corner of his mouth.

"I'm Detective O'Dwyer," says the tall man. "And this is my partner, Detective Hoskins. We'd like to ask you a few questions about the robbery and killings at the Slater and Morrill Shoe Company." The shock must have shown on Assad's face, "Am I a suspect?" The tall detective laughs, but not convincingly. "Of course not, we just want to ask a couple of questions about some men."

"I understand," Assad says, holding the door open wider. "Please come in. Can I get you both something to drink?" The short cop—Hoskins—grunts, which Assad takes to mean 'no'.

"No thank you, we're fine," says O'Dwyer, as he reaches into his shirt pocket for a photo, which he holds out to Assad to review. "Do you know this man?" Assad couldn't believe he was looking at the face of Bartolomeo Vanzetti. "Yes, he's a friend of ours; of me and my wife."

"Your wife being ….Frances Assad," says the short cop, speaking for the first time as he looked at his notebook. Somehow it bothered Assad that the detective had his wife's name in his notebook. "That's right," Assad replies.

Detective O'Dwyer continues. "And am I correct that this man… Bartolomeo Vanzetti… had dinner at your home a few months back?" Assad hesitates briefly. "That's correct. We had just met and he mentioned he was also from Italy, as my wife is, and because he had no family, we invited him to dinner." The short fat cop grunts again. Assad stares at him, now with annoyance.

"And at this dinner," O'Dwyer continues, jotting down notes in his own notebook. "Was there any discussion of any plans he might have had; what was on his mind?" Assad shakes his head, "No, mostly just talk about back home." O'Dwyer nods and without looking up asks, "Did he mention meeting with someone named... Sacco?"

"No, the name doesn't ring a bell."

"Nicola Sacco?" Assad pauses. O'Dwyer notices the pause and looks up from his notebook at Assad. "Does the name sound familiar?"

"He did mention someone named Nicola... but no last name," offers Assad.

"Is your wife an anarchist, Hajjar?" This question coming from Hoskins' beefy lips gives Assad a start. "Excuse me?"

"Didn't she work for some radical groups in South America, stirring up trouble?"

Assad was starting to get angry. "Of course not, she worked to help get woman the right to vote. I don't think that makes her an anarchist." Hoskins reply was merely to do another grunt, perhaps this time only louder. "What are trying to imply...?"

"Nothing, nothing, Mr. Hajjar," soothes Detective O'Dwyer, putting away his notebook. "We're just trying to put the pieces of a puzzle together." He takes his partner's arm and leads him to the door. As they exit Assad hears Hoskins' voice dripping with undisguised sarcasm. "Yeah, have a good night."

"Look at this rubbish!" Frances screams as she throws the latest edition of *The Quincy Patriot* on the kitchen table, almost knocking over Assad's cup of coffee. The headline yells BRAINTREE BANDITS ARE LOCATED. Assad picks up the newspaper and silently reads the accompanying story. After finishing he looks up at Frances with wide eyes.

"They think Bartolomeo, and his friend did this horrible thing? I don't believe it."

"That's because it isn't true!" she huffs, pacing around the kitchen floor. "It says they have all this proof, but to me it sounds like just a bunch of words! And, of course, the fact that they are Italians and immigrants doesn't help them." She stops and looks at Assad. "Besides," she continues. "I looked in

Bartolomeo's eyes, and what I saw was *not* the eyes of a killer!" She sits down and takes Assad's hands in hers. "We have to help him," she implores.

"I agree, my love," Assad answers. "But how?"

Frances stands up. "Some of my good friends at the Women's League—Danielle Ciccone, Inez Gallo, Maria Vespaziani—we are going to start a defense fund. Inez's husband owns an empty storefront at 256 Hanover Street in Boston. He said we can use it." Assad could see she was caught up in the moment. He had not seen her this animated since Khalil's death; although he wasn't 100% sure that was a good thing.

As Frances put the defense machinery into full gear, pulling in more and more volunteers convinced the wrong men were being held, Bartolomeo Vanzetti and Nicola Sacco were formerly indicted on September 11, 1920 for the South Braintree murders. It would take until May 31, 1921, over eight months later, for the trial to officially commence under the watchful eye of Judge Webster Thayer.

For over a month as the trial commenced, Frances and her volunteers marched up and down in front of the courthouse brandishing signs against the injustice they felt was unfolding inside, which was witness after witness either giving false testimony or recanting on previous testimony. For instance, a ballistics "expert" said the bullets fired at the scene of the crime were "consistent" with having been fired by a pistol owned by Nicola Sacco. But it was believed the witness was implying that Sacco's was the actual gun that fired the bullets, though there was no real evidence of it having done so. As a matter of fact, another expert said Sacco's gun did not fire the bullets. Then another day a cap found at the scene was put into evidence, but it turned out the cap didn't fit the pair.

Still, despite the overwhelming evidence implying Sacco & Vanzetti could not have committed these heinous crimes, on the evening of July 14, 1921, the jury returned with a verdict of guilty of murder in the first degree. Both men were sentenced to be executed.

It was felt by many—both immigrants and academics—that the two men were actually being tried for their perceived anarchist beliefs rather than for the crime they were being charged with. A storm of protest arose, with Frances as one of the main advocates. Motion after motion was introduced over the next six years into higher courts, all to be turned down by the decision-makers. But Frances' strength never wavered as she wrote letters and organized rallies, often with her three daughters at her side. But it would be to no avail.

On April 9, 1927, now knowing there was no way the execution would be called off, Bartolomeo Vanzetti stood and addressed the court for the last time, as Frances stood in the back of the courtroom, her eyes red with tears.

This is what I say: I would not wish to a dog or to a snake, to the most low and misfortunate creature of the earth—I would not wish to any of them what I have had to suffer for things that I am not guilty of. But my conviction is that I have suffered for things that I am guilty of. I am suffering because I am a radical and indeed I am a radical; I have suffered because I was an Italian, and indeed I am an Italian; I have suffered more for my family and for my beloved than for myself; but I am so convinced to be right that if you could execute me two times, and if I could be reborn two other times, I would live again to do what I have done already.

As the August 23, 1927 date for execution neared, protests broke out all over the country, specifically in New York City and Philadelphia. On August 21, a massive rally took place on Boston Common, with reports of up to 20,000 demonstrators.

Despite all the protests and rallies, there was no stopping the legal machinery and on August 23, 1927, Nicola Sacco and Bartolomeo Vanzetti were put to death while Frances Hajjar sat in the darkness of her bedroom and openly wept.

The funeral was held several days later at Langone Funeral Home as thousands followed the caskets down the street to a final burial site at Forest Hills Cemetery in Jamaica Plain. At the gravesite, Frances, Assad, Tecla, Inez and Lydia were given a prime location. Tecla and Inez stood on each side of Assad, and a now 18-year old Lydia held on to her mother's hand. As the graves were attended to, all could hear a beautiful voice off to the side, giving a stirring rendition of *Ave Maria*. Lydia looked at the source of the singing and saw a handsome young man in a dark suit singing in a most beautiful voice. He had dark hair and thick bushy eyebrows. Lydia tugged at her mother's hand. "Momma, who is that singing?"

Frances looks over, using her free hand to shield her eyes from the bright sun. "That's the son of a woman who worked with me in the Defense Fund," says Frances. "I think his name is Eugene."

Lydia stares at the man with the soaring voice. "I think he's very handsome."

CHAPTER 14

September 1938

Quincy, Massachusetts

Just over 10 years had passed since 18-year old Lydia Concetta Hajjar first set eyes on the young man singing so beautifully at the graves of Nicola Sacco and Bartolomeo Vanzetti on that humid August day in 1927. She was formerly introduced to Eugene Vespaziani after the service by Frances, and right away the two young people clicked. What followed would be a year-long fairy-tale courtship; cozy dinners, sunset walks along the beach in South Boston, even a Red Sox game or two.

They married in an intimate ceremony in Milton in June of 1928, at a small church not far from the home on Eaton Street in Milton where Eugene lived with his mother. The newlyweds agreed that it would be best to move into his house until they could afford a place of their own, as Eugene was pulling in small but decent wages singing at church services in the Boston area.

It was a good idea… until it wasn't.

Soon after moving in Lydia confided to Frances that she felt more like hired help than a daughter-in-law, and that her day was an endless ordeal of cooking and cleaning. She felt trapped she explained between sobs, speaking often with her mother on the telephone from a local drug store as she was not allowed to use the phone at Eugene's house.

Lydia hoped the situation would improve upon news that she was pregnant. But even during term she harbored suspicions that her husband was stepping out on her with others, as often the phone would ring and when she dared to answer it she would hear giggling before the caller hung up. She decided to stay at her mother's house the last few months of the pregnancy. Sadly, whereas she hoped being pregnant would help their marriage, it only worsened when the baby died in childbirth, serving only to weaken her resolve and strengthen her husband's verbal abuse (he never struck her, however).

While all this was going on, Assad observed Frances becoming more and more bitter, often to the point of stomping around the house screaming bloody murder every time Lydia called crying on the phone. He often felt helpless.

Those 10 years that passed had also not been kind on Assad. In 1929, just two years after the funeral of his friend, Assad's position at the Slater and Morrill Shoe Company terminated as the Great Depression gripped the nation and put millions out of work. People with no jobs had no money to buy shoes, so he was told. Several years of unemployment would pass before he was able to land a job at the New York, New Haven and Hartford Railroad in South Boston, ironically the very train that brought his family from New Jersey to Massachusetts. The work was back-breaking and Assad was no longer a young man. Plus, he had noticed he'd been smoking more cigars lately and drinking maybe a bit too much *arak*, a strong Mediterranean liquor. On more than one occasion he had to stop what he was doing and catch his breath.

A few months after the death of the baby, Lydia—who now to Assad seemed as fragile as Frances—came home to live with her parents at their house on Hancock Street in Quincy. Her sisters, Inez and Tecla, now with their own families, would visit often, listening to their sister's tales of misery while married to Eugene. Sometimes when they were all together at the house they would hear a car going by filled with laughing people, the driver honking his horn and waving out the window. Tecla would swear it was Eugene driving by, taunting his wife unmercifully.

The low point of this relationship, as if it could get any lower, occurred when Frances returned home one day from shopping and found Lydia sprawled on the couch, semi-conscious. Her left arm dangled on the floor, a half-bottle of sleeping pills lay on the rug just beneath her fingers. On the verge of hysteria, Frances called her physician, Dr. Gallivan, and as she waited for him to show up she tried everything to keep Lydia awake.

By the time Dr. Gallivan showed up on Frances' front steps, Lydia was already semi-awake, having vomited pretty much all of what she had taken.

"Frances," Dr. Gallivan urges. "You should really think about having Lydia treated for her mental condition. I know a well-respected psychiatrist…" But Frances cut him off angrily. "No! There is nothing wrong with her brain… it is her heart which is damaged, thanks to that son of a bitch. He did this to my sweet girl! If I had him here right now…"

"Okay, Frances," the doctor says as he tries to calm her down. "I am sure you know what to do that is best for Lydia." Frances looks down at Lydia. "I do," she says softly under her breath. "I know just what to do."

Assad, now working 10 hours a day at the railroad yard trying to pay the mortgage on the house, had no idea what his wife was planning to do.

One September night in 1936, Assad had just completed the late shift at the railway yard. Walking into the kitchen he saw a page torn from *The Boston Globe* lying on the kitchen table, he automatically assumed it was left over from Frances' lining of a cat litter box being used by a kitten she had bought Lydia with the intent of helping her spirits. But had Assad, now bone-weary and hungry, looked a little closer at the torn page he would have observed an advertisement for the sale of a .38-calibre pistol, to be sent mail-order from a store in Chicago. But his attention was focused more on a roast beef sandwich Frances had left him in the ice box. And he was famished.

Fortunately for Frances there was no one home but herself when the postman had her sign for a package that morning in late-October. She thanked the postman, went into the kitchen and put the package on the table. It wasn't particularly heavy, which kind of surprised her. She looked at the package for a full five minutes before grabbing a pair of scissors and cutting the string. She took out the contents, which was wrapped in corrugated paper. Unfolding the paper she stared at the first revolver she had ever seen up close. It was shiny silver with a leather grip and a chamber capable of holding six bullets; five of which she hoped she wouldn't need. Bullets were included in the $29.95 she sent to Chicago. It was a bargain.

Suddenly coming to the frightening realization that her husband or children might come through the door at any moment, Frances felt a ripple of panic work its way down her spine. Where to hide the gun until she devised a time to use it? Her mind raced through possible locations before coming to a halt at the most obvious; the attic. It was the one place no one would look for anything, let alone a .38-calibre revolver. She quickly re-wrapped the gun in the corrugated paper it came in. Realizing she needed to hide it more, she looked around for something else, letting her eyes settle on a dish towel she had recently used. She wrapped the gun in the soiled towel and then placed everything in a brown paper bag. Feeling satisfied, she transported her possession up to the attic, where she then tucked it up on a shelf sitting just below a rusted pipe. Satisfied that her mission was successfully accomplished, she went downstairs to start prepping for dinner.

A little over two years later, as Frances sat at her kitchen table drinking a cup of coffee on the morning of Wednesday, November 16, 1938, she scanned, as older folks do, the death notices that ran the full page of *The Boston Globe*. It wasn't long before her attention was put on full alert by a death notice with the bold heading **VESPAZIANI, Oreste**. Seeing that it was the cousin of that pig, Eugene (she proceeded to spit on her kitchen floor; with every intent to clean it up later), she read the notice intently until she found the information she needed. The funeral would be held Friday morning at St. Mary's Church on Crescent Street in West Quincy, with burial immediately after in the Church's rear cemetery.

Knowing how close the Vespaziani's were as a family, there was no doubt in her mind that the man who ruined her beautiful daughter's life would be in attendance. And how ironic she thought, while taking another gulp of coffee, that he should die in a cemetery. Feeling satisfied with her thoughts, Frances finished off her coffee, went over to the sink to rinse the cup out, put it in the strainer, and then proceeded to climb the stairs up to the attic as she softly whistled *Ave Maria*.

It is a clear and cool day the morning of Friday, November 18, 1938 as the Vespaziani family solemnly walks into the graveyard from the church with every intent of burying a loving cousin. Frances stands behind a tree off to the side, her hand inside her large pocketbook. She can see Eugene approaching, flanked on both sides by his sister, Fernanda, and brother, Raymond. There are possibly 50 other mourners following behind. When Eugene was no more than 10-12 feet away Frances emerges in front of him, pulls out the pistol and shouts as loud as she can in Italian, "YOU OUGHTTA BE IN THE GROUND, TOO!" The gunshot sounds like a cannon in the quiet cemetery as the bullet tears into Eugene's chest. He appears in shock, taking only a moment to look down at the blood that is blossoming on his white shirt before collapsing on the ground. Fernanda screams and falls off to the side as mourners scattered in all directions.

Just as Frances prepares to fire once again, Raymond throws himself at her, knocking her hard to the ground as the gun flies out of her hand and clatters along the walkway. Frances looks up and sees murderous rage in Raymond's eyes, but before he can exact any revenge on his brother's shooter, he hears his sister yell for help and he rushes back to assist some of the mourners who are trying to stop the blood from pumping out of Eugene's chest. In a daze, Frances stands up, brushes the dirt from her coat, and proceeds to calmly exit the cemetery. As she walks down Cross Street to a nearby phone booth, she can hear the wail of police sirens off in the distance. She calmly walks into the phone booth and calls Lydia, telling her in a calm voice what she had done for her, then hangs up the phone and waits in a nearby drug store for police she knows will eventually come.

She is there less than 10 minutes when a man in a long overcoat walks into the drug store. He stands over Frances, who is sitting peacefully in a folding chair. The man respectfully removes his hat. "Ma'am… are you Frances Ersillia Hajjar?"

200

She looks up at the man. "Yes," she replies. "I'm Lieutenant Cahill, Quincy Police," he answers politely. "I am here to take you to police headquarters for the shooting of Eugene Vespaziani."

"How did you know I was here?" she asks.

Lt. Cahill takes a small notebook from his coat pocket and reads from one of the pages. "A Mr. DiBona of 96 Crescent Street phoned the police to report that a woman just shot a man in St Mary's Cemetery and she fled the scene to this drug store." He closed the notebook and put if back in his coat pocket.

With that information, Frances rises and allows the officer to lead her to his patrol car. Before getting into the car, she looks at Lt. Cahill and asks, "Is he dead?" Cahill answers, "No ma'am... I don't believe he is." To that her only reply is, "What a pity."

At Quincy Police Headquarters, Frances is formerly charged with assault with intent to murder by Sergeant Theodore Young. The sergeant then transports Frances over to Quincy Hospital to be officially identified as his assailant by Eugene Vespaziani, who is in pretty bad shape. At the hospital they are met by Dr. Richard Ash, the attending physician, who gives Vespaziani a 50-50 chance to live. He says he is afraid to remove the bullet, which crashed through the chest and ricocheted off a rib around the lungs and lodged against the spine.

Frances is led to the foot of the bed where Eugene, his voice croaking in pain, identifies the woman in front of him as the shooter. "She's crazy! She's been crazy ever since I divorced her stupid daughter!" With that Frances musters all the saliva she can and lets loose with a great gob of spit that hits Eugene directly in the face; "You dirty skunk! You ruined my beautiful daughter's life!"

With that Frances is taken back to jail and held on $20,000 bail while authorities awaited the outcome of Eugene Vespaziani's injuries. While in custody, Frances is visited by her daughters Lydia and Tecla, though Inez had decided not to visit. Assad visits as often as possible, promising her he would pray every day for her soul. Frances tells him he doesn't look well.

Eleven days after Frances' bullet crashed into Eugene's chest, her former son-in-law succumbs to a serious infection that developed around the wound. The medical consensus is that the infection was caused by rust that had accumulated on the bullets as a result of being stored for two years in the attic near a rusted pipe. As a matter of fact, the gun was so rusty the police were surprised it fired at all.

Upon the death of Eugene on November 29, 1938, Frances Ersillia Galliotti Hajjar is charged by District Attorney Edmund R. Dewing with murder in the first degree. After a lengthy court case that ran just over five months, and in a crowded courtroom at Norfolk Superior Court, on April 12, 1939, Frances is found guilty of murder by Judge Frank J. Donahue. The judge gives Frances a life sentence which will be carried out at the Sherborn Reformatory for Women. Sitting in the back of the courtroom, Tecla and Lydia let out an anguished wail, Raymond and Fernanda Vespaziani hug each other and silently weep, and Assad just hangs his head and prays. He looks up as Frances is being led out of the courtroom. As she is, she turns and looks at Assad, mouthing the words, *"I love you."*

Assad feels Tecla's soft hand on his shoulder. "Poppa, we talked about it and we think it would be best if you came to live with me and my family in Braintree." Assad looks up at her but says nothing. "The kids would love to have you around, and with Lydia working so many hours at her new job, it's going to feel very lonely at the old house. Please Poppa." All Assad can do is nod his head okay. Together they leave the courthouse, heartbroken and feeling alone.

CHAPTER 15

April 1941

Braintree, Massachusetts

Living the past two years without his beloved Frances is taking its toll on Assad, both mentally and physically. Although he makes it a point to visit her several times a week, always with a promise to pray for her soul, it is getting harder and harder to make the three-hour round trip to Sherborn. Plus, the job at the railroad yard isn't going that well and he has been laid off.

With more time on his hands Assad finds himself smoking and drinking more than he usually would. He has also put on weight, which isn't helping his deteriorating condition. It seems like every time he plays with Tecla's children he finds himself becoming more and more out of breath.

On the morning of April 28, 1941, Assad is shaken awake by Tecla. "Poppa, wake up, it's Momma!" Still half-asleep, Assad quickly asked, "Momma, is she here?"

"No Poppa," Tecla says softly, helping her father out of bed. "She is sick. They said they are sending her to Medfield, to a hospital there." Assad swings his long legs over the edge of the bed—he had taken to sleeping in his trousers—and Tecla helps him get his feet into his shoes. She ties them tightly and helps him up. "Come on, we have to go," she says.

It took close to an hour for Tecla and Assad to make the journey to Medfield State Hospital, where they are met by Inez and Lydia. But it would be too late. They are told by a doctor that Frances had suffered a massive stroke in prison and was rushed over to the hospital. Sadly, Frances passed away minutes after being admitted. Assad asks the doctor if they could see her one last time, and he said they could.

Standing around the hospital bed, Tecla softly sobs, Inez seems in shock, and Lydia has her head buried in Frances' chest openly crying. On the other side of the bed Assad kneels at the side railing, putting his hands together and praying for a miracle he knows can never happen.

On a chilly April morning in 1943, two years after the passing of his wife, Assad Hajjar, now 70 years old and not in the best of health, sits in his car in Tecla's driveway, having just journeyed out to get some milk, bread and another box of cigars. The heater in the car pumps softly creating a fog on the inside of the windows. Assad has the radio tuned to WBZ-1030AM and listens as morning man Carl DeSuze recaps not only last night's Red Sox game but a breakdown on how the troops are doing fighting in Europe and in the Pacific.

Having heard all he wanted to hear, Assad shuts off the car engine, rubs his left arm a little, grabs the bag of groceries and heads for Tecla's back steps which lead into the kitchen, making sure not to wake anyone in the house who would surely still be sleeping this early in the morning.

As soon as Assad puts his foot on the bottom step he feels like his chest has just exploded as intense pain shoots through his body like a raging beast. The bag slips from his grasp and on to the driveway as he grasps the railing to try and steady himself. The pain subsides enough for Assad to sit halfway up the stairs as his breathing becomes jagged and erratic. Just then another wave—more a tsunami—of pain wracks his body one more time, and suddenly Assad feels the world start to darken, as if a large cloud had suddenly passed in front of the bright morning sun.

Strangely, as the morning becomes darker and darker, the pain becomes more tolerable, or maybe it just doesn't matter as much. For whatever reason (*darker and darker*), Assad, sitting on his daughter's back steps while life oozes slowly from his body, begins to think about what his life has meant to him and the people that were part of that life; about the roles they all played.

Even as the intruding darkness descends upon him, Assad can make out the faces of:

His father, also Assad: *"Go my son, and become the best man you can be. Help others. Keep your faith strong. And always remember how much we love you."*

Father Abbott: *"Ten long years ago you came to us in the dark of night, a frightened boy, lost and alone. But we all watched you grow into an incredible young man, one who saw his calling and embraced the teachings of our Savior."*

Father Pietro: *"It appears the Holy Father wishes to have Assad meet with him at the Vatican."*

Pope Pius X: *"This is a Holy Relic. Something you must always treasure."*

Chaim Stern: *"Miriam and I came to this country with no one. We never had any children. But in the brief time we have known you, and Frances and the children; you have made us all feel like family. And family, for my people, means everything."*

But the one face that seems to linger longer, and with more clarity than all the others, is that of Captain Giovanni Galliotti. It was that day aboard his ship in the Port of Messina, where he met his true love for the very first time. And now, content to let go and join her, Assad stares up at the blue heavens and remembers the words uttered with great pride by Captain Galliotti:

"Father Assad Hajjar, this is my daughter, Frances Ersillia Galliotti. *Mia Piccola Rosa."*

As Assad Hajjar lays back on the stairs and closes his eyes for the last time, a small smile emerges on his face as his lips form the last word he would ever utter:

"Ersillia"

The End

Epilogue

Kathy Anderson

Living through the writing of this story has been an emotional ride for me. It was a "bucket list" item of mine for sure!

I wish I had met my grandparents; Assad and Frances. I often think of what we would have talked about and how I would tell them how lucky I was to have them for grandparents.

But the story you have just read doesn't end with Assad's death in 1943. Everyone's life still went on, as lives do no matter what hand the past has dealt.

My Aunt Tecla and her husband, Peter, moved from Peach Street in Braintree and lived in three other houses in Braintree. They raised their five daughters, and in 1955, after one daughter married in Braintree, they all moved to sunny California. Peter worked for the railroad and it seemed likely that railroad work in Massachusetts was not reliable. That was the reason offered for the move, but deep down I truly believe Tecla wanted to move as far away as possible from the shame of what her mother had done. Lydia, my mother, was crushed when they moved. She felt very alone without having her sister, Tecla, close by. Even though I was very young, I remember how sad that day was.

My Aunt Inez and her husband, John, lived in Quincy and raised four children. They lived in the same house for many years and hardly ever talked of the past. I have fond memories of my Aunt Inez. She was a very kind soul and a very sweet lady.

My mother, Lydia, worked in the O'Connell Shoe Factory in Braintree. By the time she reached 30 years of age she had already been married and divorced, lost a child at birth, and saw her mother die in prison after serving three years of a life sentence for the murder of Lydia's ex-husband. That's the burden she lived with.

But happily, her life took a turn for the better.

Bill Anderson was a relative of one of our neighbors. At the time stationed with the U.S. Army in Guadalcanal, someone in Bill's family wrote to him that Lydia was now "available." So Bill promptly wrote to Lydia and, eventually, that correspondence led to a romance. When Bill came home from WWII, he married Lydia in a civil ceremony in Braintree. My brother Robert was born in 1945 and I came into the world in 1948.

My parents and my brother and I had a very happy life in many ways. Living in Braintree, my father knew everyone. My brother was a star Little League baseball player and I was a happy Campfire Girl. We had good times. And life definitely improved for my mother.

My father was a happy-go-lucky, simple man of faith. He worked for the Town of Braintree and in 1957, while widening Liberty Street, a tree being cut down fell on him. My father was in the hospital for almost a year while recovering from the accident. Lydia was once again thrust into another of life's low blows. But my father survived, and my family carried on.

Lydia was left, in many ways, quietly sad and permanently scarred from the events of her early life. But it did not prevent her from being a good wife and a great mother. I learned life's wonderful lessons from my mother Lydia. I appreciated her guidance, humor and wisdom.

My mother passed away in 1993 at the age of 83. Subsequently, her sisters Tecla and Inez passed away after both living into their 90's. It was the end of three women who belonged to a generation of strength. Sadly, my brother Bob passed in 2003. He would have been proud of this book.

Fortunate was I for having known them all. In life it is wise to remember and to recognize the hand of Divine Providence in all things. My life has been and continues to be a result of this belief. **September 2020**

A photo of my mother, father and brother in front of my Aunt Tecla's home in Braintree on the morning of my brother's First Communion in 1953.

Pictured: Lydia Concetta Anderson & Bill Anderson; Robert Anderson (age 7) and Kathleen Ersillia Anderson (age 5).

Made in the USA
Middletown, DE
22 August 2023

37090643R00119